Poisoned

Poisoned

Sue Mayfield

Hodder
Children's
Books

A division of Hodder Headline Limited

Copyright © 2004 Sue Mayfield
Published in Great Britain in 2004
by Hodder Children's Books

The right of Sue Mayfield to be identified as the Author of
this Work has been asserted by her in accordance with the
Copyright, Designs and Patents Act 1988.

1 3 5 7 9 10 8 6 4 2

All characters in this publication are fictitious and any
resemblance to real persons, living or dead, is purely
coincidental.

A Catalogue record for this book is available from
the British Library

ISBN 0 340 86064 2

Typeset in Palatino by Avon DataSet Ltd,
Bidford-on-Avon, Warwickshire

Printed and bound in Great Britain by
Bookmarque Ltd, Croydon, Surrey

The paper and board used in this paperback are natural
recyclable products made from wood grown in sustainable
forests. The manufacturing processes conform to the
environmental regulations of the country of origin.

Hodder Children's Books
a division of Hodder Headline Limited
338 Euston Road
London NW1 3BH

To Hannah, with love

Acknowledgements

Thanks to Anne (for her knowledge of Edinburgh) to Tim (for loving support and cups of tea) and to Hannah (for liking the first draft more than *Voices*!) Thanks also to Emily at Hodder and my agent Elizabeth Roy.

A Note About Labyrinths

The Labyrinth visited by Isabel and Alice in Chapter 42 is modelled on a real event which toured cathedrals in Britain during 2002/3. 'Walking the Labyrinth' is based on an ancient style of praying and can be a moving and powerful experience. (I've done it three times and I recommend it!) For more information visit www.labyrinth.org.uk

1

ISABEL

Let me tell you a story . . .

Once upon a time, there were two girls who were best friends. They were inseparable – like two sides of a coin. They were a double-act. French and Saunders. Ant and Dec. Itchy and Scratchy. They were soul mates. Almost like sisters. Then one of the friends did a terrible thing. Something unforgivable. And then? Well, and then they weren't friends any more. What did you expect?

I should be having a lovely time. Here I am in the south of France, in blazing sunshine, beside a turquoise pool. But I'm miserable.

"Make sure you've got plenty of cream on," says Mum, lolling on a sun lounger beside me. I take the top off a tube of suncream and squirt thick white tracks of it down my arms and legs. I'm fair-skinned you see. I burn easily.

Macy doesn't have that problem because she's dark, with olive skin that tans as soon as the sun so much as peeps out of the clouds. Macy should have been in France too. That was the plan. A week in the sun at the end of a busy summer. But, as you can see, she's not here. She cancelled at the last minute, too late to get her money back. Not that I feel sorry for her. Anyway, it was a bargain flight – Manchester to Nice for only £35 – so it's not a big deal.

Mum suggested I bring someone else. Someone to keep me company. But who else is there? Macy's been my best friend for over a year. It narrows your options, having a best mate. You end up with nothing but a circle of casual acquaintances. Billy No-Mates. Do I sound bitter? Well don't blame *me*!

I nearly asked Chloe Stretton, but I wasn't sure sun loungers and French cuisine were quite her thing. She's more into chips and black leather. Alice – my older, wiser sister – is somewhere in Italy, inter-railing with a couple of mates from uni. So there's just me and Mum . . . and Pete, my stepdad.

Right on cue Pete does a belly flop into the deep end and showers us with sparkling raindrops. Mum squeals and dabs herself with a beach towel. Pete thrashes energetically across the pool and climbs out looking like something between a walrus and a rhino, a roll of freckled flab hanging over the waistband of his trunks. He puts wet hands on Mum's hot shoulders and she squeals again. Like they say, three is a crowd.

But, I'm wandering off the point . . . You wanted

to hear about Macy, didn't you? My sometime friend. Well, what shall I tell you? Macy Paige is American. She comes from Vermont. Did you ever try that Ben and Jerry's ice cream flavour called Full Vermonty, with maple syrup and chunks of caramel? Macy's addicted to it. She says she has to eat it to maintain her cultural identity! Not that she's been over here that long. She came when we were in Year Eleven. Now we're in Year Twelve – except they don't call it that in our school, they call it Lower Sixth. Actually we're in Upper Sixth now – or we will be in a week's time, in September. So that's what – all of seventeen months? Seventeen months, one week and two days, if you really want to know.

Sometimes when people arrive new in school, they ease their way in gently, like someone getting into an icy swimming pool bit by bit – gradually, so they don't notice the cold. Not Macy. She just jumped right in – hit the place like a tornado. She joined the drama group, the orchestra, the choir, the school council. She was loud and confident and opinionated – just the way everyone always thinks Americans are supposed to be!

I was bowled over by her. We clicked from the word go. We were so different and yet so alike, so on the same wavelength. Like me, Macy loved singing and dancing. Like me, she wanted to go to drama school and work in the theatre. Like me, she loved cities and parties and movies and shopping and sitting in Starbucks drinking cappuccino. (Macy would have loved the shops in Nice, and all the pavement cafés too.) We liked the same music too – Dido and Nina Simone and Nelly Furtado. Strong women with fabulous voices. Macy's got a fabulous voice – or at least she likes to think she has. (No, that's tight! She has.) She wants to be a jazz singer, and she has lessons with a woman called Milly.

The only thing we didn't have in common was our taste in men – then. She never liked Jamie, that much was obvious. And I failed to see what she saw in Phil Colvin. Worse – Macy had a crush on our English teacher, Mr Kempe, all the way through Year Eleven and *he's* going bald!

Year Eleven is a lousy time to arrive at a new school. I don't know what her parents were thinking of. Macy came in March and we had our GCSEs in June. She had to work flat out to catch up on syllabuses and get her head round the English school system. It's just as well she's smart.

Mum hands me a bottle of Orangina, cold from the fridge. The glass is misted like frost on a window. I take a long swig and stretch my legs out in front of me. I'm reading a trashy novel that I found in the apartment. It's a historical romance, a real bodice-ripper. Hermione What's-her-face (posh, rich, dressed in pearls and lace, daughter of Sir Henry Something-or-other) is falling in love with her poor, thin, underfed – but strangely handsome – piano teacher, Gabriel. Her father (pompous, red-faced, pound signs in his eyes) wants her to marry Edward Something-hyphen-something (who is loaded but dull). I can tell you for certain, she isn't going to. She's heading for ruin. She'll run off with the penniless piano teacher and her father will disinherit her. Then the piano teacher will leave her for a buxom violinist and she'll starve in a draughty attic with her sickly, snot-nosed baby. (I could write this stuff myself!) Actually Hermione should marry neither of them. She should walk away and keep her dignity intact. Become a nun or something.

Okay, so I sound bitter. Like I said, that's not really my fault.

The piano teacher has blue eyes – "*blue as the sea in summer*." (How clichéd is that?) The sea on Rimsay was mostly grey. Duncan said it would be different in summer.

2

MACY

What did Isabel say about me? Did she blacken my character? Did she say it was all my fault? I should put my side of the story, shouldn't I? Set the record straight. So, what d'you wanna know?

My name is Macy Paige. I am seventeen years old. I was born in Richmond, Vermont, which is in the United States – about two hundred fifty miles north of New York City. I came to England two years ago – almost, because my dad got a research job at Manchester University. (He's a biochemist.) We live in Manchester in a big cold house that's a hundred and fifty years old, near a park with oak trees. My mom is a financial consultant with HSBC Bank, and I have one (younger) brother called Ethan who is a skateboarder with poor personal hygiene. I am five feet tall and weigh one hundred and forty-five pounds. Okay, so I'm a little overweight. I eat too many choc chip muffins. (My dance teacher tells me to wrap my thighs in plastic bin liners so I sweat and shed as I dance. I tell her to go take a walk.)

You wanna know about Isabel? She's cool. (Did you expect me to diss her? Come on!) Isabel's a very talented lady. She can sing, she can dance, she can act. She wants to make movies and I reckon she's got what it takes. She'll probably make it. She's clever, too. And attractive – even if she does look a bit like Geri Halliwell (*before* the yoga videos!).

We were friends. Really good friends. When I first arrived here from the States I was like, "Hello, excuse me, would someone show me what I'm supposed to be doing here?" Isabel helped me out. She took me under her wing, as they say – looked after me. She introduced me to the Drama crowd, got me tootling my flute in the school band, showed me where to get my hair cut and my legs waxed and my eyebrows shaped – a girl's gotta know these things!

I like Isabel. We've been through a lot together. I know her about as well as you could know anyone. I mean, we've shared a flat together all summer. We even shared a bed for some of the time – when we were at her mum's cousin's. But don't go getting any ideas! Isabel snores like a hog! You wouldn't expect it would you? She looks so dainty and sweet.

Snoring's not her only fault. You want me to tell you about some others? She has plenty – but then, who doesn't? Okay – she's unbelievably untidy. And when she washes the dishes she always leaves the really dirty ones to soak in the sink. "Soak them overnight," she says, and then she leaves them there a whole week. She always squeezes the toothpaste from the top so it looks like a wrung-out flannel –

which would be fine if she used her own tube, but she always forgets hers and has to borrow mine.

Okay, I know. These are minor character flaws. You want something juicier? Go to hell! Isabel Bright is my friend. *Was* my friend.

Alright then, if you insist . . . Sometimes she takes herself too seriously, and sometimes she's a bit of a drama queen. Sometimes she says tactless things she doesn't mean, and sometimes – no, almost always – she walks into a room and expects every guy there to think she's gorgeous. That's annoying. But what is more annoying is that they nearly always do.

Duncan thinks she's gorgeous. Or at least he did. I don't know what he thinks now. You could tell he was nuts about her by the look on his face. Smitten, that's what I'd call him. Head-over-heels smitten. So why did it all go so pear-shaped? (What is it about pears and disaster? Why is pear-shaped supposed to be bad? *Pears* are pear-shaped. *I'm* pear-shaped. Pear-shaped is nice . . .)

3

DUNCAN

I was gobsmacked when I found the bottle. All sorts of crap washes up on the beaches of Rimsay all the time – shoes, rope, TV sets, polystyrene packaging, and bottles – shampoo bottles, Coca-Cola bottles, beer bottles, even Bacardi Breezer bottles. But a Bacardi Breezer bottle with a message in it? That was a first.

The message was written on the back of a Silk Cut packet rolled up like a cigar and stuffed into the neck of the bottle. I had to prise the lid off with a stone.

This is what the message said: *"If there are any half-decent blokes out there who aren't axe murderers, egomaniacs or Britney Spears fans please contact Isabel Bright . . ."* Then it gave her address. West Clarendon Street, Manchester.

I could only just read it. It was streaked with sea water, damp and smudged.

I wrote to her straight away. Maybe that was a mistake. Maybe I should have left it where I found it on the shore – on a slimy belt of seaweed, beside a dead herring gull. But it seemed so amazing, so momentous. Isabel says it was only a joke. She never expected anyone to find it. She didn't even write the message herself. Her sister Alice wrote it. But still . . .

So I wrote a letter – the first one in years. I told her all about myself. That my name was Duncan MacLeod. That I lived on the Isle of Rimsay – which is in Scotland, in the Western Isles. That I wasn't an axe murderer and that I thought (think!) Britney Spears is pants.

And she wrote back. Surprisingly quickly.

That was how it started. How we started to get to know each other. By letter at first and then by e-mail. We'd meet in cyberspace and chat – about Shakespeare (I was doing English A Level, she was playing Miranda in *The Tempest*), about our families and our pets (she had a cat that could crawl commando-style, I had a goat that ate trash), about our lives (hers was exciting, mine was pretty dull). We told each other a lot of things – about our dreams, our secrets, our likes and dislikes. She was into dancing and parties and trendy cafés. I was into lobster and beaches and Crunchie McFlurrys.

Alright, so we didn't have much in common, but I liked the sound of her anyway. Besides, aren't opposites supposed to attract – like magnets? And she must have liked me a little bit or she wouldn't have kept on writing.

I had no illusions. We were just friends. She was seeing someone called Jamie, then. She'd tell me all about him – creep that he was. How they'd been an item, and then he'd dumped her and broke heart. How they were thrown together again because he was in *The Tempest* too – as Miranda's lover Ferdinand, in fact – and how he wanted to give it another go.

She'd write me these long e-mails as if I was an agony aunt or something. Should you forgive someone if they say sorry and ask for a second chance? Did I believe in love at first sight? I wrote back as if I was an expert. If only she'd known!

It seemed an amazing coincidence that she was in a play about an island when I lived on one, so she'd ask me about Rimsay. What did it look like? What kind of stuff did I find on the beach? What did it feel like being surrounded by the sea twenty-four seven? I sent her some shells to wear in her hair in the play and a boxload of seaweed to put on the set. Perhaps the seaweed was a bit over-the-top. My mum thought I was mad when I sent it.

Isabel asked me to send a photo of myself. She said it was for her friend, Macy, because she wanted to know what I looked like. (Macy did. Not Isabel.) I sent a really cheesy shot that Ned took after I won the table-tennis tournament. I looked hot and sweaty and I had this ridiculous Craig David beard that Angus had dared me to grow. She must have thought I looked a right pillock. She never said so.

4

ISABEL

The timing of Duncan's accident was very strange. In fact it was downright spooky. It was October. A Saturday night. The last night of our three-night run of *The Tempest*.

There I was on a stage in Manchester, acting the part of Miranda – weeping, as I watched an imaginary ship wrecked in a terrible storm. "*A brave vessel . . . dashed all to pieces . . .*" (Are you impressed that I can still remember my lines ten months later? You're not? Fine, be like that!) Anyway, at the exact same moment, in the freezing waters of the North Atlantic, just off the coast of the Isle of Rimsay, Duncan MacLeod was clinging to an overturned fishing boat – clinging to his life, in fact – while *real* waves crashed over him. How weird is that?

They were sure he must be dead. Statistically, he should have been. He was in the water for eleven hours and he was unconscious when they found him. It was another five hours after I phoned before the helicopter picked him up. His mother sounded frantic.

Me phoning him that night was a bizarre coincidence too. I'd only phoned him one other time before – ever – and that was on Macy's mobile for about three seconds, to ask him about some guitar stuff he'd asked me to send. That I should call him at *that* moment, that day of all days . . . It was as if I was *meant* to ring him or something. Like destiny – if you believe in stuff like that.

I was in a pretty bad state when I made the call. It was late at night. Talk about emotional rollercoasters. First, there was the play. The last night was something of a triumph. Everything went right. I was on a complete high and everyone was telling me I was wonderful. (I believed them too, which was a mistake – don't they say pride comes before a fall?) Then there was the cast party, which was all very luvvie and gushing – speeches and bunches of flowers and all that jazz. And then, just when I was thinking that life couldn't get much better, Jamie dumped me – for the second time. Just like that. Said he didn't think things were working out. He didn't feel the same about me anymore. He'd *thought* he was still in love with me . . . but actually he wasn't. Soz etc.

I was in a taxi when I phoned Duncan. I was crying so much I had dribbly snot dangling from my nostrils. (You know the sort?) Why exactly did I phone? Did I just want to hear his voice? Was he my comfort blanket – like the bit of frayed wool with a grey satin edge that I used to suck on in bed? Or did

I want him to ride into my life and rescue me, like Rapunzel in the tower? Was I hoping he'd be my knight in shining armour? Either way, when his mum told me he was missing in a storm, I felt guilty and selfish for thinking *I* was the one who needed sympathy. And I felt sick – paralysed with worry and fear.

Is it true that losing someone makes you realise how much you value them? Or is it just the case that the sadness of loss (or the fear of the sadness of loss) fools you into thinking you care about someone more than you really do? All I know is that when Mrs MacLeod phoned next morning to say they'd found him – alive, I was so happy I wanted to burst. I felt like I'd been reborn. Given a second chance.

So I hopped on a train and went to Glasgow – where they'd taken him in a rescue helicopter. Alice came with me, on her way back to university. She came as far as the hospital lift. Then I walked along the corridor to the ward by myself, feeling like I was on the brink of an adventure.

It was the first time we'd ever seen each other. He didn't have a clue what I looked like or that I was about to arrive at his bedside like Florence Nightingale. I only recognised *him* because his name was on the door. He looked nothing like the photo he'd sent me on-line. He was lovely. Much lovelier than I'd expected. But then, maybe I was biased.

Anyway, he looked at me – this mad staring stranger, standing in his hospital room – and said, "Are you lost?" and I said, "No, I'm Isabel," and then he smiled this fantastic smile.

I don't know now what I think about love at first sight. Duncan once said he believed in it. The plot of *The Tempest* falls apart if you *don't* believe in it because the play only has a happy ending if Miranda loves Ferdinand and she's only known him three hours by the time they reach the final scene. Expert as I now am in such matters (ho-ho!) it seems to me that love is a complicated, gangling thing that grows bit by bit and is both very tough and at the same time terribly fragile. It's something you *do* rather than something you feel. Something enormous and life-changing.

But I definitely believe in *attraction* at first sight. And when Duncan smiled at me from his hospital bed, I knew we were more than friends.

5

MACY

If you ask me, Isabel fell for Duncan on the rebound. Jamie Burrows messed her up big style. "Put her heart in a blender and pressed *frappé*" as Jim Carrey's friend says in *The Mask*. (Do you know that movie? I love it!)

Isabel and Jamie had already been an item for a year when I arrived in the UK. Then it was on and off all through Year Eleven and into the Lower Sixth – mostly on, despite all my efforts to make Isabel see sense. They say love is blind, and she was blind alright. Blind to what a shallow, two-timing jerk he was/is/always will be! I told her she was playing with fire to go out with him a second time over. But would she listen? She said he was different, nicer, more mature. Yeah, sure Isabel. Like I believe you!

What really bugs me is she *said* she and Duncan were just friends. For months, that was the line she spun me. He was her e-friend, her cyber pal; he was just a mate. Actually, I say that was what she told me, but the truth is for the first month or so she didn't tell me anything. She kept the whole thing a secret. All the stuff about the bottle and his letter and their late-night chats and the bag of shells . . . What sort of best friends keeps stuff like that to herself? I mean, come on, babe, this is juicy gossip! This is better than *Sex and the City!*

When I finally got to hear about Duncan (shame about the name!) she made out that she was only writing back because she felt sorry for him. He was a sad bored lonely guy stuck on an island in the middle of nowhere. She was too nice not to answer his mail. Like he was a charity case or something and she was Princess Diana!

She let me read the messages he'd sent – eventually – and I told her, "Isabel – this guy is NICE!" He *was* nice, I swear. Even an idiot could tell that. He was warm and funny and kind and sympathetic. But no, he was just a guy, just a friend. He didn't mean *anything* to her. Jamie was her true love. It was Jamie Jamie Jamie.

Granted, Jamie is nice looking – if you like that sort of thing. I mean, we're talking *Pop Idol*, here. Perfect teeth, big puppy eyes, hair gelled into neat little peaks. We're talking Gareth Gates. Which is fine when you're ten – but Isabel, babe, grow up!

So one minute they're just friends and she's saying if *I'm* so interested in Duncan (Dunkin Donuts I called him – it's a fast-food chain in the States. Oh, you knew that? What, they have them here? Where? Show me! I want donuts dipped in chocolate sauce NOW!) then I'm welcome to him. Yes, she really did say that. She said I was welcome to him. Talk about changing your tune, lady!

He sent her a photo on-line. I kept badgering her to ask him what he looked like. Well, *I* wanted to know even if she didn't! I told her to tell him the photo was for me. Frankly, when I saw it I thought he didn't look great. He had the sort of rosy red cheeks that the Sixth Form rugby team have – when they've had sixteen pints too many! Maybe it was just a bad photo. Actually he looked a bit like Darius – before he shaved his Italian waiter beard off. Before anyone thought he was sexy. When he just looked a bit silly.

Isabel made me take the photo home with me. I thought it was a bit weird that *she* didn't want it. He was *her* friend. Not mine. But then it wasn't the most flattering portrait. I took it to keep her happy and when I got home I put it in the bin. What did you expect me to do? Pin it on my bedroom wall?

6

DUNCAN

She didn't look like I expected her to. I mean, I'd never asked her what she looked like or requested a photo or anything. That was way too corny and, anyway, it would have looked like I was coming on to her, wouldn't it? So I'd just imagined her – like you do. I suppose I'd pictured her a bit like – what's she called in *Planet of the Apes?* – Helena Bonham Carter. Not the monkey suit, obviously, but the dark hair, the fine chiselled English Rose face . . . I have to say, I'm more a brunettes man than a blondes man, really. But Isabel was blonde. And tiny. Petite. Big nose. Perfect teeth. Not unattractive – don't get me wrong! Just not what I was expecting.

And she hadn't warned me she was coming. I mean I might have changed my boxer shorts if I'd known I was about to have a visitor! Suddenly she was just there – in the hospital ward, smiling at me. I hadn't a clue who she was. She didn't look like a nurse – she was a bit too casually dressed – denim jacket, stripey gloves, hair in two plaits like Britney in the *Baby, Baby* video – you know the one? (Not that I like Britney or anything.) So I asked her if she was looking for someone and she said no, she was Isabel.

Isabel. Even then the penny didn't drop straight away. Well, I *had* just had a near-death experience. I wasn't exactly at my sparkling best.

She sat down by the bed – and then it dawned on me. Isabel! Doh! I was touched that she'd travelled all that way. I mean, Manchester isn't exactly round the corner from Glasgow, is it? She'd brought me a Yorkie Bar too, which was sweet of her. Appropriate too, since high-energy, sugar-rich snacks are what they stuff you full of when you're recovering from hypothermia.

It wasn't the most romantic meeting. Not how I'd have planned it exactly. For starters, I must have looked pretty awful. Mum says I was blue when she first arrived at the hospital. By the time Isabel came, I reckon I must have looked greyish – like death warmed up. Literally warmed up. That was what they did to me when they got me to the hospital. They did "core rewarming" – like putting a frozen chicken in the microwave!

So, Isabel sat by the bed and looked at me. I think she might even have held my hand – but that seems a bit unlikely now, when I think about it. Then she told me that Jamie the Wonder Boy had dumped her a second time. I hope I didn't smile too much. I have to admit I was deliciously happy to hear it but I tried to sound sympathetic. She didn't look *too* heartbroken – but then I'm not the world's most experienced person when it comes to traumatised women. I've led a pretty sheltered life so far, really.

She only stayed half an hour. We ran out of things to say after the first ten minutes. A nurse that looked like Dawn French came and took my temperature and poked me a bit, and when she saw Isabel she said, "Is this your girlfriend then?"

I was embarrassed, to say the least, so I said, "You'd better ask *her* . . ." Why did I say that? Why didn't I just say No?

Isabel didn't say anything at all and the nurse smiled knowingly as she hung my clipboard on the bottom of the bed.

After Isabel had gone, the same nurse came back again. When she saw the empty chair she said, "Is that your girlfriend away then?"

"She's not really my girlfriend," I said, but she just winked at me with an *Oh yeah, yeah, yeah!* sort of look.

I have to confess, I hoped she was right and I was wrong.

I was in hospital for ten days. Once they'd got me thoroughly rewarmed and all my organs were functioning again, they sent me home to Rimsay. (No helicopter this time – just the ordinary aeroplane, splashing down onto the beach.)

That was when things hotted up with Isabel. I was off school for another couple of weeks. She phoned me every day – sometimes more than once. And she sent me things – chocolate, plectrums, cute little home-made cards. She even sent me a hot-water bottle with a fluffy cover on it like a teddy and a note that said, "Just in case you start to cool down again." Cool down? Not likely!

The calls got longer and longer – and the phone bill got bigger and bigger. Then I had this mad idea to invite her here for New Year. Hogmanay on the Isle of Rimsay. How could she resist?

I never thought she'd actually come . . .

7

Okay, so I'm a hopeless romantic. My expectations were ludicrously high. I was hoping for island magic and singing seals. Duncan had described stretches of milk white sand ("Like the Bahamas without the palm trees," I think he said) and carpets of wild flowers and schools of dancing porpoises. To be fair, he'd also told me about the wind ("Strong enough to flay the shell off a tortoise!") and the fact that everyone on the Isle of Rimsay was mad from too much sea and sky.

My only previous experience of Scotland was our *wonderful* (note the heavy sarcasm) holiday in Ardnamurchan, where I sent my message in a bottle – a week in the middle of nowhere with only a load of birds and my weird family for company. I'd thought Arnamurchan was bleak, but Rimsay was worse. There was *nothing* there. Duncan says islanders drink a lot of whisky. I'm not surprised. I'd hit the bottle after a week!

He was right about the sand, though. That was the first thing I saw as we came down out of the clouds – a great expanse of milky-white, edged with sea. The aeroplane – which was more like a mini-bus with

...unged down onto the beach and landed in
...er of spray.

...s I walked across a layer of crunchy shells,
...he sun was shining and I felt excited and hopeful.
Duncan was there in an enormous grey jumper with
a collar that rolled right up over his ears. He gave me
a hug and kissed the top of my head.

No proper kiss. Shame. In my head I'd pictured us
in a full-frontal snog – movie style – with violins
playing in the background. Instead, Duncan quoted
a line from *The Tempest* – one of Caliban's lines about
the island being full of strange noises – and then
suddenly there were all these cows walking onto the
beach, bellowing. Well, it was original!

We rode in the post bus (think Postman Pat's
van without Jess). There was Scottish folk music
twangling on the radio and the seats smelt strangely
of whisky. Duncan sat beside me but he didn't put
his arm round me or anything. I felt a bit sick after
the flight – a bit woozy, the way you feel when you
step off the waltzer at a fair. Thank god I didn't throw
up on his shoes, is all I can say. We travelled through
tracts of nothingness – lumpy moon rock, yellow
grass, sheep all over the road. Ten minutes into the
journey the sky clouded over. By the time we reached
Northton rain was spitting against the windows
of the bus. Okay, so Duncan hadn't promised me
sunshine.

Northton was just a string of houses along the edges of a rocky shore and Duncan's house was at the end of the string. It was grey and squat and looked as if it had taken some hammer from the weather. Duncan showed me my room – his brother Neil's room with a cheery knitted blanket on the bed and a pile of neatly folded towels – and the bathroom, which was at the end of the landing. Then he made bacon sandwiches and cups of watery Nescafé.

Okay, so I suppose I should have realised that feeling close to someone in cyberspace (feeling that you can say just about anything in an e-mail or a text, or even on the phone) isn't the same as feeling comfortable when you're actually *with* someone in the flesh. But I was surprised how awkward I felt with Duncan. It was as if being five hundred miles apart was actually easier than being two feet apart. I felt self-conscious and clumsy, and I couldn't think of anything to say.

We stood in the kitchen waiting for the kettle to boil. Boris, Duncan's dog – who was ugly and stank like rotten seaweed – kept bringing me a rubber ring to play tug-of-war. When I took hold of it, my fingers got covered in drool.

"Sorry," said Duncan. "He smells a bit!"

A *bit*?

After we'd eaten, we sat in his bedroom, rain

drumming against the front of the house. What was there to talk about? I knew all his secrets already. Knew what he thought about just about everything. He showed me his guitar, strung with the new strings I'd sent him from Manchester. He showed me his table-tennis trophies and his five-a-side football championship medal.

Then I showed him my photos of *The Tempest*. Me as Miranda with cheesecloth dress and shells in my hair.

"Rimsay shells," said Duncan, squinting at the photo. "They look good."

Sebastian Reeves as Prospero, in a velvet cloak with shards of mirror stitched to it.

"Made by me," I said.

"Very nice," said Duncan.

Me in a passionate clinch with Jamie Burrows. "We'll skip over that one," I said, putting it to the bottom of the pile.

"Yuck! Ferdinand!" said Duncan, looking over my shoulder. "I hate him!"

"Me too!" I said. (Don't look at me like that! I *do* hate him!)

When we came to the photos of Macy – Ariel in combat pants and facepaint, Ariel singing to Ferdinand, Ariel dancing about playing a silver xylophone – Duncan looked very closely at them. Too closely, if you ask me.

"She's better looking than you made out," he said, casually leafing through the pile of photos.

"I never said she was *bad* looking," I said.

"You said she was a cross between Bjork and Ruby Wax . . ."

"So?"

"Well, one of them is weird and the other is old," he said.

"But they both have dark hair," I said.

"True," he said. He was still looking at the pictures of Macy.

"And they're both small with big bottoms," I said. (Bitch!)

"Big bottoms are fine," Duncan said. I blushed. He was smiling at me. Mine isn't exactly small. (More J-Lo than Kylie.)

Thankfully we were spared any further discussion of Macy's anatomy – or mine – by the arrival of Duncan's mum, who knocked loudly on the door as if we might be up to something. I wish!

I'd kind of imagined Duncan's mum and I would be pals. We had, after all, both fretted the night away when Duncan was lost at sea. I hadn't bargained for how frosty and fierce she'd be. She looked a bit like Miss Trunchbull off *Matilda*. I sat through supper wondering if I'd get sent to the chokey if I didn't eat all my food.

Eating up all my food was actually a pretty tall order. Mashed potato, baked beans and this strange greasy sausage in squares. My portion was enormous – much more than I usually eat. (I'm more a salad and pasta girl really.)

As we ate, Duncan's mum asked me lots of questions about school and my family while his dad grunted unintelligibly over his plate of mashed potato. I began to think that maybe Mum and Pete weren't so bad after all.

Then there was Duncan's grandpa, who lives with them and is pretty ga-ga. He asked Duncan's mum three times during the course of the meal who I was and when I was leaving. Duncan caught my eye across the table and I had to stare at my plate to keep from laughing.

After supper we watched TV. What else was there to do? I was cold and had a headache from the flight. I wanted a hot bath and a proper cup of coffee but instead I had to sit through a whole episode of *Holby City*. Later, when *Graham Norton* came on, Duncan's mum got up and changed the channel. "Not that horrible little man," she said, scowling. "He talks nothing but filth!"

8

DUNCAN

Isabel really didn't see the island at its best. I wanted her to come in the spring, when the wild flowers are in bloom, but I was worried things would cool off between us if I waited that long to invite her. Maybe we should have stuck to meeting on the mainland. Maybe it was too early in our relationship to expose her to my strange family. Grandpa can't help what he says. (He's got Alzheimer's disease.) But Mum and Dad? I thought they could have made a bit more effort!

For the first twenty-four hours I was convinced I'd made a big mistake. She came two days before New Year. The first evening was a bit grim. No doubt she's told you about *Holby City* and my mum's cooking. She has? I won't bore you with my version then.

The next morning, on the Thursday, we went for a walk round the bay to Kerravore. I wanted to show Isabel the Singing Sands. There's this beach on the north of the island where, in the right weather conditions, if you press your ear to the ground you can hear this whispering, wailing sound. My grannie used to tell me it was the voices of drowned sailors buried under the sand. (I wet the bed over that one for weeks!) Needless to say, a windy day in late December wasn't the right weather conditions. The sand was too damp to lie on and the wind was making such a racket that you couldn't hear yourself think.

"It really does sing . . . sometimes," I yelled at her above the roar of the waves.

"I believe you!" she shouted back. I don't suppose she did, really.

I felt like a magician whose tricks were all going wrong.

On the way back it came on to pour and we got soaked. Isabel didn't really have the right sort of clothes for Rimsay. She had on a skimpy denim jacket that stopped halfway up her back and these suede boots that let the rain in. She didn't seem too happy when we had to jump across a stream partway along the beach and she got her feet wet. I suppose it's fair to say that Isabel isn't really an outdoorsy type. But then, she'd told me that from the outset. She's a city girl. She likes bars and shops and sophisticated nightlife. She told me she hated mud in her very first letter to me. So why was I dragging her along squelchy cliff-top paths, for heaven's sake? (Meet Duncan MacLeod – he *really* knows the way to a girl's heart!) She looked freezing too. When we got back she needed a hot shower but the nurse was in, giving Grandpa his weekly bath, so she had to make do with towelling down her hair and dipping her feet in the kitchen sink.

If I said there wasn't much to do on the Isle of Rimsay that would be the understatement of the year. If you don't like scenery or fishing, and the beaches are drenched in rain, then you're a little stuck. After our unsuccessful walk there was only one thing for it – table-tennis in the village hall. So that was where we headed after lunch. Isabel was starting to look a little moody and miserable so I phoned Ned, my best mate. I reckoned having him there would help things along a little. How wrong a man can be!

Ned arrived as we were putting the net up. He gave Isabel a kiss on the cheek – which seemed a bit overfamiliar for starters. I'd barely touched her all day. I wasn't sure she fancied me now she was actually within touching distance and I didn't want to come on too strong if she was having second thoughts.

"What do you think of Rimsay?" Ned said, taking off his wet coat and flinging it on the floor. I don't know what Isabel was about to say – something polite but untrue, probably – but Ned came straight in before she had time to open her mouth and said, "Bloody dump isn't it? I can't wait to leave!"

Ned's such a poser sometimes. Of all of us, he's the least likely to leave the island. On a good day he says there's nowhere he'd rather be.

Isabel was smiling as if she agreed with him, which annoyed me. Well, Rimsay might be a little low on entertainment but it *is* my home. Today, when I went with Dad to get the lobster pots up off the reef, there were porpoises – a dozen or more of them – swimming just off the point at Kerravore, and the evening sun was catching the hills making them glow like coals. Listen to me! Duncan MacLeod – poet laureate! All I'm saying is Ned was oversimplifying things for effect. When I leave – which inevitably I will (what is there for me here?) – it will be a huge wrench. Part of me wants to stay on the island for ever. It's more complicated than just wanting to get away to the mainland as quickly as possible. Islands have a great power over you. Surely someone who's played Miranda should know *that*.

"Duncan's planning on staying here," said Ned, dismissively. "Frau MacLeod won't let him off the island!"

Ned had this thing about my mum being strict – like a concentration camp guard in a Second World War movie or something. I know she can be a bit – how shall I put it? – abrupt, but the way Ned was milking it you'd have thought she was the bride of Hitler. He was trying to wind me up. I didn't rise to the bait.

Ned had handed Isabel a bat and they were knocking up. Isabel was pretty useless, as I'd suspected she might be. Not that being good at ping-pong is a big deal. In fact, great table-tennis skills are tantamount to an admission that you've had a sad and sheltered childhood, let's face it!

Ned started talking about Hogmanay, which is what we call New Year in Scotland. Did they have it in England – in Manchester? (He kept saying "Manchester" with a really embarrassing Liam Gallagher accent, and Isabel giggled every time he said it.) Did she realise Hogmanay was just an almighty excuse for a piss up? Was she a whisky drinker?

Then he really landed me in it. "I hope you're going to be a civilising influence on Duncan this year, Iz," he said. (Who said he could call her "Iz"?)

"Why's that then?" she said. She was scrabbling about in the corner trying to retrieve the ball from under a stack of chairs.

"Because last New Year he got *very* drunk and made a bit of a fool of himself," Ned said. Isabel served the ball across the net. She was looking at him wide-eyed with curiosity. He ended up under— (Surely he wasn't going to tell her *that*!)

"Two-five!" I said, announcing the score really loudly to cut Ned off mid-sentence.

Ned picked the ball up off the floor and threw it to Isabel.

"Under what?" she said, smiling.

I was eyeballing Ned but he was enjoying himself too much to hold back.

"Under the table with my cousin Kate," he said.

Isabel shot me a look. I wasn't sure whether it was a jealous stroppy look or an *I'm impressed* look. Like I say, I'm not the best judge of women.

"Kate, the drummer in the band?" she said.

Thanks Ned. Thanks for telling Isabel that.

"Yeah, but it was nothing serious . . ." I didn't finish the sentence. When you're in a hole, stop digging.

Isabel lost the game spectacularly – four points to twenty-one. Then she played me. But Ned hadn't finished embarrassing me. He sat on the window sill, swinging his legs, making daft remarks. Had I shown Isabel my five-a-side football medal? (What if I *had*?) Did she know I had a six inch scar on my thigh from an accident on my bike in Primary Three? Had she tasted my mum's fish pie yet? When was she going to invite me (*us*, I think he actually said) to Manchester? Had I done my party piece yet?

"Party piece?" said Isabel. She was losing ten-nil. I was trying to hit the ball off the table just so she'd get a point.

"He can belch the first four notes of Beethoven's Fifth," said Ned. (No, I *won't* demonstrate for you!) That time any idiot could have read the look on her face. It was disgust. Pure and simple.

"Thanks, Ned," I said. "I'll do the same for you sometime!"

"What?" he said, coming over all innocent. "I was only making conversation!"

The game ended twenty-one to two despite my best efforts to massage the score in Isabel's favour. I played Ned and beat him twenty-one to nineteen. Then we tidied away the nets.

"Will you be coming to the practice?" Ned asked her, as we were putting the bats in the cupboard.

"Practice?" said Isabel.

"For the gig," Ned said. We were playing a set at the Hogmanay bash. Me and my band, the Posh Porpoises.

"We're rehearsing this evening," I said. "I wasn't sure you'd want to come."

"They're pretty good," Ned said. "But then I'm biased. I'm their manager."

"I know," said Isabel. "Duncan sent me a tape. I really like them. I'm looking forward to the gig." She was smiling at me. Maybe I hadn't blown it totally. Maybe she still liked me a *bit*.

"Which track did you like the best?" Ned said. "I'm a big fan of the Britney cover version, personally."

"I liked *Port in the Storm* the best," Isabel said. She started humming it quietly. Then, without looking at me, she said, "I had it in my head the night you were missing." She'd never told me that. I was touched.

Port in the Storm is an acoustic number. Angus, our bass player, plays cello on it. It's more mellow than our usual stuff – more romantic.

"Did Duncan tell you he wrote it about *you*?" Ned said suddenly.

That's not strictly true. I did write it after I found the message in the bottle, but it isn't really about me – it's fictional. And the girl in the song (*"You're my port in the storm . . . the coat that keeps me warm . . . you're my shel-ter . . ."*) well, she's imaginary. Sort of. Well, maybe she's Isabel too. I don't know. It's art isn't it? Who knows where the ideas come from? . . . But, what the hell! Isabel was smiling at me – *really* smiling at me – for the first time since she'd arrived on the island.

"He wrote it after you started e-mailing him," Ned said, switching out the lights. (Come back Ned!, All is forgiven!)

As we left the village hall, I slipped my arm round Isabel's shoulder and she took a step closer to me and wrapped her arm around my waist. Oh yes! Things were definitely looking up . . .

9

What do the Posh Porpoises sound like? I'd play you the cassette, except I destroyed it when we got back from Edinburgh. I unspooled all the tape till it looked like a great bundle of tangled ribbon. Then I chucked it in the bin. Okay, so that was a bit silly. But then I was upset, wasn't I?

Duncan described the band as a cross between Travis, Ash, Oasis . . . and Iron Maiden. I think they sound a bit like Coldplay. They do a mixture of cover versions and their own stuff. There's a guy called Angus who plays bass (and sometimes cello) and a guy called Ross on the keyboard. Then there's Kate on the drums, and Duncan on guitar and lead vocals. Kate and Ross are pretty average. But Angus is good and Duncan is very good. Duncan's got a great voice and he moves well too. He's got what our drama teacher, Ms Redman, would call "stage presence" – "the X-factor", as Pete Waterman would say. Maybe he'll take it further when he goes to university. Join a new band. Write some hit songs. Maybe he'll end up as a teen icon. Now that *would* be weird. How would I feel about him then? How do I feel about him *now*? I'm still working that one out . . .

The Hogmanay bash was fantastic – not least because Duncan had finally started acting like we were a couple. He introduced me to people as "My girlfriend, Isabel – all the way from England!" and he kept beaming at me with this big, goofy, crinkly smile. It felt like the entire population of the island of Rimsay was at the party. I met Duncan's uncles and aunts and cousins and former babysitters, his English teacher, his music teacher, his GP, his table-tennis coach – even the midwife who'd delivered him. *Duncan MacLeod – This Is Your Life!*

There was ceilidh dancing with a pipe-and-fiddle band – which Duncan was really good at – and some daft party games. (I volunteered to shave a balloon, covered in shaving foam, that Duncan was holding between his teeth – and, yes, I succeeded without popping it.) And then there was food, followed by forty-five minutes of the Posh Porpoises live on stage. People danced, and a couple of twelve-year-olds tried to crowd surf and broke a beer glass. I sat at the side of the hall, drinking rum-and-coke and glowing with pride. Duncan looked great. He'd let me put styling wax in his hair, which really suited him, and he had on the new black T-shirt that I'd bought him at Diesel in Manchester. It's fair to say that I fancied the pants off him.

When midnight came there was bagpiping and *Auld Lang Syne* (which I can never work out the words to) and a countdown to the new year. And kissing. At last – our first proper kiss! Two minutes long at least – with tongues.

Was he a good kisser? Yeah, he was pretty good. Was he as good as Jamie? That's an unfair question – Jamie and I had had years of practice. Duncan was a relative beginner. But it was a damn good start . . .

My last day on the island was perfect. It was sunny, for starters. The sea was turquoise with gleaming white surf. Duncan took me to Triagh Mor, which is a vast beach. I filled my pockets with tiny pink shells and we paddled in the sea – which was like ice. Duncan showed me the exact spot where he had found the bottle. "Here," he said, and he bent down and kissed the sand, the way the Pope kisses the tarmac when he steps off an aeroplane. I laughed.

We walked all the way along the beach as far as the rocky headland. It was pretty cold, but I didn't care because I was wearing Duncan's massive grey sweater and he had his arms round me.

At the point, where the sea crashed against the cliff in plumes of spray, we saw seals – not singing, admittedly – but swimming and visible to the naked eye. As we stood on the rocks watching them, Duncan kissed me. It was, without a doubt – the best kiss yet. He tasted of salt and sunshine. As he kissed me he ran his fingers through my hair, and when we finally stepped apart he looked at me and said, "God, Isabel, you're beautiful you know . . ."

10

MACY

The thing about Isabel is she's EXTREME. Things are either totally wonderful or they're totally crap. There's no in-between state – no half measures.

When she came back from visiting Dunkin Donuts on his desert island, things were Totally Wonderful. (Note my capital letters there.) She wasn't just "dating" Duncan or "seeing him", she was like madly and utterly in love with him. It was like, Duncan did this . . . Duncan said that . . . Duncan, Duncan blah-blah-blah! All this from the girl who'd spent six months saying he was just a guy, just a friend, just someone she happened to be writing to.

I had to listen to these descriptions of dolphins and singing sands and carpets of pearly pink shells. And I'm like, "Am I really hearing this?" The way she talked about the island you'd have thought it was somewhere in the Caribbean. Some little tropical paradise with silver sand and a sparkling ocean – like that place in *The Beach* with Leonardo de Caprio. (Did you see that movie?) Or Bali. But we're talking Scotland here. Not famed for its glorious climate.

Before she went she was like, "Duncan says it'll be cold. Duncan says it'll be windy. Duncan says there's cow shit on the beach." I have to say I couldn't really picture her there. I mean Duncan sounded sweet enough but cow shit and Isabel? Uh-uh! Isabel isn't really your survival kind of girl – and we're talking windswept Hebridean island in the middle of winter. I imagined Rimsay a bit like that place on *Castaway*. Not the movie where Tom Hanks is in a plane crash and he goes bonkers and ends up talking to a football. (Good movie – a little long perhaps, but I liked it. Good performance from Tom – he should have got an Oscar in my opinion.) No, I mean that TV show where they dumped a load of weird people on an island for a year and they all argued a lot and got upset about killing the chickens. Now that *was* windy. And they all walked about in big jumpers with no make-up and greasy hair. Can you really see Isabel Bright coping with that? Come on, Isabel is an urban chick. And she's clean. She's a two-showers-a-day girl and she never likes to be more than six inches away from lipstick and a mirror.

I have to say, I was kind of surprised when she came home so ecstatic about it all. She didn't even seem to mind that she'd ruined her new suede boots by stepping in a bog. You mean, she cared about this guy more than her shoes? My god! This really *was* love.

Isabel's one for details. What I didn't know about that guy's bedroom, his wardrobe, his on-stage persona, his taste in food, his friends, his kissing technique – after a week of listening to her, wasn't worth knowing. I felt like I knew every inch of his body without having ever clapped eyes on him. Every last scar and freckle. Every little smooth/ hairy/kissable morsel of him. And that's weird. Surely you agree? Weird.

11

ISABEL

So it was January. New year, new term. We started rehearsing a play called *My Mother Said I Never Should*. It's a four-woman play about a daughter, a mother, a grandmother and a great grandmother – and how they do and don't get on. I was the mother, Jackie. Macy was Margaret, the grandmother. We had to fight a lot, which was fun. Not that we'd had much practice at that stage. We hadn't anything to fight about (until recently).

Sebastian Reeves, who's used to getting all the best parts in plays we do at school (he was Prospero – my dad – in *The Tempest*), was really miffed that there were no boys' parts.

"It makes a change," said Macy. "Four decent women's parts. It's more than Shakespeare ever wrote." Macy has this thing about Shakespeare being sexist. She's got a point. In *The Tempest* there are fourteen roles for men and only one proper women's part – Miranda. Macy played a spirit (Ariel) who was kind of – what's that word that means both sexes together? – androgynous. And all the other girls in the drama group had to perform in drag – stick-on beards etc.

We were in Starbucks after a rehearsal, drinking cappuccino and eating chocolate muffins. Macy and I used to spend a lot of our time drinking cappuccino, when we were friends. Last year I spent most of my allowance in Starbucks, Coffee Republic, Costas, and La Viva – which is this little place round the corner from our school. We'd go to a café when we left rehearsals, or in our free periods (if we could get off the school premises without being spotted!), and we'd just chat – about the play, about school . . . about Duncan, sometimes.

To be honest, Macy wasn't that interested in Duncan. She never said as much, but whenever I mentioned him – told her something he'd said on the phone, or showed her a card he'd sent me, or described something we did when I went to visit him – she got this bored look on her face. Or she'd change the subject. You'd have thought she would have been pleased for me, wouldn't you? I wouldn't have been like that if *she'd* been seeing someone . . .

12

DUNCAN

I wouldn't recommend a long-distance relationship. It's expensive, for a start. I got a job earlier this year – when I turned eighteen – serving behind the bar at the Seabay Hotel – and during the time when Isabel and I were an item, most of my wages went on train fares and phone credit! It's time-consuming too. I spent hours on-line chatting to Isabel when I should have been revising for my A Levels, and sometimes we'd text each other – what? – twenty times in a day. But then, if she'd been on the island, I would have been spending time with her. Real time, not virtual time. So I would have been just as preoccupied. More so.

The truth of the matter is, if Isabel had been on the island I probably wouldn't have been able to keep my hands off her. After I finally got round to kissing her at the New Year's party, she came on pretty physical. It was a bit overwhelming, to be honest. Don't get me wrong. I fancied her like crazy. But it was a bit much. It was like driving a car too fast with no brakes.

She seemed to know what she was doing. I don't know if she and Jamie the Wonder Boy actually slept together. She didn't tell me either way. Did she tell you? (Actually, no, don't answer that. I don't think I want to know.) I once started to ask her but she got in a strop with me – and Isabel in a strop is something to avoid at all costs.

Whether they did or they didn't, I was certain she was *way* more experienced than I was. Which was a bit scary. Exciting, but scary.

Being five hundred miles apart slowed things down a bit, obviously! Don't they say "absence makes the heart grow fonder"? I'm not sure about that. I'm not sure I liked her *more* because she wasn't there. But I certainly didn't like her any less. It was my idea to meet up in Glasgow the weekend of her birthday.

13

MACY

We were in the sauna when she told me. I was laid on my back on the hot boards with sweat trickling down my cleavage. (What? You didn't want to know that? Well, thanks!)

"What have you got planned for your birthday then, babe?" I asked her. I was hoping we might go out somewhere, since her birthday was going to be on a Saturday. Last year we all went for a curry – Isabel and me and Jamie and Jamie's friend, Ig, and Chloe and Phil and Rosie . . . the usual crowd. The drama gang.

"I'm going to Glasgow," she said. She said it really casually, scooping a ladleful of water onto the coals, which hissed and gave off that lovely good-for-your-lungs smell.

"Glasgow?" I said. Why was she going to Glasgow? (Bit slow on the uptake there, Macy. Wasn't it obvious?) I played dumb anyhow.

"Who are you going to Glasgow *with*, Isabel?" I said.

She didn't answer. She didn't need to. She just smiled and crossed her legs in the lotus position.

"He's flying there for the weekend," she said. "It's

all booked. He's paying for it with his bar wages."
She was sitting up straight with her back against the
wooden wall.

"A whole weekend? Just the two of you?" I said.

She nodded, a big grin spreading across her pretty
little face.

"And where are you staying?" I said.

She smiled to herself, eyes closed secretively, not
answering.

I kicked her with my toe. "Isabel," I said. "Tell all!
Are you staying in a hotel?"

She smiled again. "I don't know," she said.

"Liar!" I said. I flicked her with the end of my
towel.

"Honestly," she said, opening her eyes. "Duncan
didn't say. It's a surprise! He just said he'd sort it."

"I *bet* he'll sort it! My god!" I said. "Isabel! You're
going for a dirty weekend!"

"Ma-cy," she squealed, all innocent and prudish.
"It's not a dirty weekend. It's a romantic mini-
break."

Mini-break? Who was she kidding? Wasn't she
moving a little fast, here? I mean *meet* the guy by all
means. Go for a pizza or watch a movie or something.
But Isabel, you're only seventeen after all. My mom
would never let me spend the weekend in a hotel
with a guy I hardly know (so was *that* my problem?
Was I just plain old jealous?)

* * *

Isabel was totally excited the week before. I went with her to have her legs waxed. Normally she just goes for a half leg. I mean, who's gonna see your thighs in February? Why suffer the pain or waste the cash? But this time she went the whole hog – splashed out on the full leg and bikini-line special. Oh baby! This was serious beauty treatment! I just hoped he was worth it.

We went to Café Nero afterwards and sat by the window looking out at the street. I took a sparkly wrapped parcel out of my bag and handed it to her. "You'd better have this now – since I won't be seeing you on the actual day," I said.

"Oh, thanks, Macy," she said, taking it from me. It was small – purple hologram paper – soft and squishy. She made a big thing of sniffing it and shaking it and trying to guess what was inside.

The waiter took our order. It was a guy we know from school – Danny Bridgewater from the Upper Sixth. "Two cappuccinos," I said. "They're on me. It's a special occasion. It's her birthday – almost. Make them extra large ones."

Isabel was waving the parcel about in front of her face. "Shall I save it?" she said. "It's small enough to take with me in my bag . . ."

"No," I said. "Open it now! I want to make sure you like it."

She started to unfasten the sellotape – carefully, daintily, so she didn't tear the paper. I'd made a double layer. Wrap on the outside, then a layer of crinkly tissue inside. It made a soft rustling sound as she unfurled it.

I was dying to see her face, and I wasn't disappointed.

It was lingerie – all the way from Ann Summers. If he was taking her for a weekend in a hotel, she might as well look the part. Isabel gave a squeal and held up a pair of tiny, black, lacy panties just as Danny Bridgewater brought our coffees to the table. I'm not sure who blushed most, Isabel or him! Either way, I wish I'd had a camera.

14

We met up for my seventeenth birthday. Did Macy tell you that already? It wasn't like you think. In fact it wasn't quite what *I* was expecting. But it was nice, really nice.

I met Duncan at Glasgow airport. I was hoping to be there in plenty of time, but my train was late so I only just made it. I saw the tiny Rimsay plane touching down from a café on the airport roof. Then I saw Duncan. He looked lovely.

Have I described him yet? Macy has? What did she say? Well, anyway, here's my version . . . He's tall (I only come halfway up his chest) and a little on the lanky side. Dark hair – quite messy, and eyebrows like that guy off the Stereophonics. He's got a lopsided grin and slightly crooked teeth and a big nose. Okay, so he's not conventionally goodlooking – but the overall effect is pretty good. And anyway, looks aren't everything. (Jamie's drop-dead gorgeous but he's a shallow, self-obsessed poser.) The best thing about Duncan is his eyes (greenish) that crease up into tiny slits when he laughs – which he does a lot!

We were both mega-nervous. When Duncan is nervous he talks really loud. "HAPPY BIRTHDAY," he said, like he was announcing it to the whole airport. Several people's heads turned in my direction. He kissed me, but we got the angle wrong and our noses bashed into each other. (How come people never do that in films?)

"I haven't got you a present yet," he said. "The shopping opportunities aren't that great on Rimsay, as you know. So I thought you might like to choose something here. Is that okay? It was either that or a tartan apron!"

"Tartan apron would have been great," I said, and we laughed more than the joke deserved.

We rode on a bus into the centre of Glasgow, to Buchanan Street. I had butterflies in my stomach. The trouble with seeing someone only now and then is every time you meet up you sort of start all over again. You have to kind of warm up – tune in, like finding a radio station on the dial. It takes a while to feel comfortable, to relax with each other. That was one thing with Jamie – we'd been together so long it was as natural as breathing.

I was especially nervous about where we would be staying and what Duncan was expecting from me. That was Macy's fault. She'd really wound me up about it being a raunchy weekend in a hotel, and she'd bought me these ridiculous thong knickers – which I confess I was wearing. (A bad idea because the lace trim was really itchy.)

Duncan hadn't told me where we were spending the night. He'd just said he'd sort it; it was a surprise. In fact we stayed in a youth hostel just off Sauchiehall Street – in single-sex dormitories with creaking iron bunk beds. Not much call for lingerie there! I shared my room with three Japanese girls who had massive rucksacks which they packed at three in the morning, endlessly wrapping their belongings in rustling plastic bags. Duncan's dorm was full of drunken Australians and one of them was sick in the corridor at five a.m. So much for a romantic mini-break!

In the morning we ate sachets of Alpen with UHT milk in the self-catering kitchen, surrounded by unshaven back-packers.

"This reminds me of home," Duncan said. "When the boat is late we drink UHT milk," he said. "U-H-T. It stands for Ultra Horrible Tasting!" he said.

But if the nights were a little – shall we say – disappointing, then the days more than made up for it. Especially the Saturday, which was my actual birthday. It was very romantic. We did tourist stuff – walked in the botanical gardens, visited an art gallery, wandered through the cathedral. I took lots of photos of Duncan grinning at me. Duncan at the Burrell Collection, Duncan on Sauchiehall Street, Duncan outside the Transport Museum. We went shopping in this mall on Buchanan Street and Duncan bought me a sparkly necklace from

Accessorize. I bought him a Crunchie McFlurry in McDonalds (they're his favourite and he hardly ever gets to eat them) and he ate it on a bench in the park, feeding me spoonfuls with the little plastic shovel.

Then we went to Starbucks. "What do you recommend?" he said, as we stood in front of the counter. I told him to go for the grilled panini with mozarella, roasted peppers and sun-dried tomatoes – which is a bit of a favourite of mine. "You don't get *that* on the Isle of Rimsay," he said, grinning.

"Magnificent," he said, wiping his mouth on a napkin as he finished the last bite. One of the things I love most about Duncan is the way he's so enthusiastic about things. Jamie was always so cool and hard to impress. But Duncan – I just have to speak, or smile and he's happy. *Was* happy . . .

We went up a great high glass tower – the highest tower in Scotland and the only tower in the world that rotates through three hundred and sixty degrees. (Are you impressed?) We went up in a lift to a viewing platform at the top and an American woman took a photo of the two of us with windblown hair.

The views were amazing. You could see down the river to the sea and north to big green mountains.

"There's the hospital where you visited me," said Duncan, pointing across the city. "And there's Ibrox stadium, where Rangers gave Man United a good stuffing in the Champions League!" He dug me in the ribs, and I giggled and pretended to care about football – which in reality, I don't. (Though I did once go with Jamie to see Man U arriving at Old Trafford on a bus after they won something or other – but only because I wanted to see Beckham!)

After dark the streets were humming. Glasgow is a clubber's paradise. There are over fifty venues in the city centre. Duncan wanted to go to the cinema because he never gets the chance to at home. (No multi-screens on Rimsay!) So we went to this arty cinema and saw a weird French film that I didn't really understand, with subtitles and lots of sex. I think Duncan was a bit embarrassed at how many times they took their kit off, but he didn't say so.

Then after the movie we went to a club called Nice 'N' Sleazy and danced to R&B. Duncan made a big effort and danced energetically, but I was worried that he wasn't really enjoying it. It's not really his style of music for starters.

"Do you want to leave?" I said. I had to yell above the beat. We were taking a break, leaning against the wall with pint glasses of water because there were no chairs free.

"No, it's fine!" he shouted. "You have fun. It's your birthday!"

We didn't stay long. I suddenly felt tired. We walked home through garishly lit streets.

"That was my first ever time in a nightclub," Duncan said, wrapping his arm around my shoulders (Imagine! He's eighteen and he's never been clubbing!)

"Did you hate it?" I asked.

"No, not at all," he said. (I love his voice. He sounds like Ewan McGregor.) "I just felt a bit of a prat – a bit of a 'hick from the sticks'. You know, goofy island boy out of his depth in the big city and all that. Like Crocodile Dundee in the middle of New York or that bit in *Greystoke* where Tarzan makes a fool of himself at a dinner party."

"I remember that," I said. "He jumps on the table and rips his chicken apart with his hands, and all these posh English people look shocked and stunned!"

"George of the jungle!" Duncan said, pounding his chest. Then all of a sudden he scooped me up in his arms – the way vampires carry fainting women in Hammer Horror films – and started running with me along the street to the hostel. I was squawking so much that a man crossed the street to make sure I was okay!

At the bottom of the hostel steps he put me down and we kissed each other. I mean, *really* kissed each other. We fitted properly by then, slotting naturally together as though we were one flesh.

"Happy birthday," Duncan murmured.

"It's a *very* happy birthday," I said, winding my fingers in the waves of hair at the back of his neck. "Shame about the dormitories."

"Do you mind?" Duncan said. He looked worried. "It's just that I wasn't sure if you'd want . . . I mean I didn't want to assume . . . And it was cheap! Basically, I'm a typical tight Scot, see!"

"Don't worry about it," I said, kissing him again to show I didn't mind. "Thanks – for a lovely day."

15

DUNCAN

I've been reading a lot of Greek myths this summer –
what with Isabel's play and everything. Everywhere
you look in this stuff, people are travelling – making
epic journeys.

Take Odysseus, for example, in *Odyssey*. He
leaves his wife, Penelope, to go off and fight the
Trojan wars. (Remember the wooden horse?) And
then, after twenty years' separation, he journeys back
to her. On the way he goes through shipwrecks
(tell me about it!), battles and storms, is blown to the
four winds, visits Hades (that's Greek hell, not
the bloke with the big chin and the blue face in
Disney's *Hercules*), sees ghosts – and finally commits
murder . . . all to get back to his love.

Or Orpheus, the guy with the lute. He travels to
the Underworld and is rowed across the River Styx –
where the souls of the dead pass from life to death –
all to be reunited with his lover Eurydice.

It's not just Greek myths either. There's *Titanic*
(which has to be one of my top-ten worst films): Kate
Winslet, ploughing along corridors full of icy water
just to get to Leonardo De Caprio. And *The English
Patient* (one of my top-ten best): Ralph Fiennes

walking miles across the Sahara to get back to Kristin Scott Thomas – only to find that she's dead. Epic journeys. Acts of heroism in the name of undying love. Crossing continents – whole worlds even . . . So, hell! Aberdeen to Manchester was nothing!

What was I doing in Aberdeen, you may well ask.

Aberdeen is my first choice university. Provided I don't totally mess up my A Levels, I'll be going there in a month's time to do English and Film Studies. There was an open day back in November – only I missed it because I was in hospital being thawed out. So I went to this special day for new applicants on a Saturday in March – and on the way back home I took a detour to Manchester to see Isabel.

Alright, so it wasn't exactly on the way. Plane to Glasgow, overnight in the Blue Sky hostel (eight quid a night, but sadly no Isabel this time), then a two and a half hour train journey to Aberdeen. A few hours looking at libraries and lecture theatres and meeting the creative writing tutor (who looked like Mr Garrison off *South Park*). Then a six and a half hour train journey to Manchester – arriving at eleven o'clock at night. But what's six and a half hours when you're in love?

Isabel met me at the station with a Crunchie McFlurry. That alone was worth the trip!

16

MACY

I went to New York in March, just for the weekend, for my grandmother's seventieth birthday. Grandma – or Moma Paige, as we call her – lives in an apartment block twenty-three storeys high in the Upper East Side. From her window you can see right into Central Park just a couple of blocks away. Sure I'm biased, but New York is just the best city. I love the buzz of it – the noise and the crowds, yellow cabs honking their horns, and steam coiling up out of the pavements, and foul-mouthed taxi-drivers yelling at each other at red lights.

It was unbelievably cold when we arrived. Piles of grimy snow were heaped along the sidewalks. Then, on the Saturday morning, all of a sudden spring came.

"You've brought the good weather with you, Macy, sweetie," said Moma Paige.

"All the way from sunny England," I said wryly. Manchester isn't exactly famous for its sunshine, now is it?

Central Park was full of joggers and children and roller-bladers and romping dogs. We bought warm bagels from a bakery on Seventy-Seventh Street and ate them on Poet's Walk. An old man was sitting on a bench feeding a squirrel French fries from a paper bag.

It was good to be back in the States again. Not that I don't like England – don't get me wrong, I love it. It's cool. But there are things I miss. Foodie things especially. Honey roasted peanuts, for example – served hot from a barrow on the street corner. They're hard to come by in downtown Manchester. Whenever we go home to the States, Mom cruises the grocery stores and delis, filling her basket with all the things we miss most – Hershey kisses and grape jelly and Oreo cookies and pickled beets. I went to Macy's department store and bought a tube of face cream – just so I could get a carrier bag with my name in big letters. It's pretty smart they named a store after me, don't you think? And not just any old store – only the biggest department store in the world!

New York is a great place to eat. I pigged out all weekend. There's this deli a block away from Moma Paige's place that sells the most amazing eat-all-you-can salads for six dollars. You get your plastic container and then you fill it up with leaves and chicken and strawberries and potato salad and hearts of palm. Oh man! Isabel is a real salad freak – she'd have loved it.

"Have you been acting lately, Macy?" said Moma

Paige, as she heaped tomatoes and parma ham into her plastic pot.

"I sure have," I answered. (I go all American when I go home to the States, although the way my grandparents talk you'd think I'd lost my accent completely. "You sound real English, Macy!" they squeal. I tell them being able to change the way you speak is a necessary skill for a wannabe movie star like me. I mean, listen! I can turn on an English accent when I have to. Just call me Gwyneth Paltrow. "We've just finished this play called *My Mother Said I Never Should*," I said, sprinkling croutons on top of my Caesar salad.

"Play with the gypsies in the wood . . ." said Moma Paige, quick as a flash.

"How did you know that?" I asked her. Those are the first two lines of the play:

> *"My mother said I never should*
> *Play with the gypsies in the wood . . ."*

All four characters are chanting that when the lights come up – me and Isabel and Chloe and Rosie Mason.

"I heard it before," said Moma Paige, picking up a load of noodles and green beans. "It's an old playground rhyme."

There's nothing Moma Paige doesn't know. She used to teach Fifth Grade and she's like a walking encyclopedia.

"And did you have a good part?" she said.

"Yeah, they were all good parts," I said. "Four good parts for women in the one play, get that."

"And your friend, Isabel, was she in it too?" Moma Paige said. She has a remarkable grasp of my social life considering I live on the other side of the Atlantic.

"Yes, Ma'am," I said. "She was my daughter."

"What fun!" she said.

We paid for our salads and left the store.

"And Isabel?" said Moma Paige, as we walked along the sidewalk. "Is she well?"

"She's in love," I said.

"Oh my!" said Moma Paige. "Is he a dish?"

I love that phrase. Like a guy's something delicious that you've cooked or something – drizzled in olive oil and garnished with a sprig of coriander!

"She seems to think so," I said. "I haven't actually met him." That was the single bad thing about my weekend in New York. I got to be away from Manchester the one time he came to visit. How is *that* for bad timing?

"Is she keeping him secret?" Moma Paige said, looking at me quizzically. We were in the elevator. I pressed the button to send us speeding upwards.

"No," I said. "He lives in the Outer Hebrides."

"I thought for a moment you were going to say he lives in outer space, then," she said and we giggled all the way up to the seventeenth floor.

17

ISABEL

It was nearly midnight when his train arrived. Manchester Piccadilly at that time of night isn't the nicest place for a girl to be. My stepdad Pete had wanted to drive me to the station – but then he'd have taken us back home and we'd have had to make polite conversation with him and Mum until they finally decided to go to bed. Duncan was only staying a couple of hours. Why waste it making small talk with parents? So I turned down Pete's offer and huddled in the platform snack bar drinking instant coffee instead.

The train was delayed. Duncan phoned me from Bolton to tell me it was running forty-three minutes behind schedule. As he approached Manchester he sent a text: *Luvly Iz. Can't w8 2 c u. XXX D*

We didn't go straight home. I figured if we arrived back after Mum and Pete were asleep, we'd have more privacy. Anyway, I wasn't tired. And the more I thought about Duncan, the more wide awake I felt! We went to Music Box on the Oxford Road, which is a club our crowd goes to sometimes at the weekend. Some of the drama group were there – Chloe and

Phil and Natalie Roberts. And Jamie. He was with Kirsty Baker, who'd bleached her hair like Christine Aguilera. Call me bitchy, but I thought she looked tarty! To be honest, I'd been secretly hoping Jamie *would* be there because I wanted him to see me with someone else. Okay, so that's a little cheap, I agree. But wouldn't you do the same?

The clubbing was a success. Duncan was more at home than he had been in Glasgow and, with a couple of Calsbergs inside him, he was well away on the dance floor. He's a far better mover than Jamie ever was.

"Just call me DJ Duncan," he said, as we threaded our way through the crush of sweaty bodies to dance again. "Come on, Isabel, this is my second time in a nightclub. I'm a regular clubber now!" I took his hands and did a bit of twirling, salsa style. We were laughing together. Out of the corner of my eye I could see Jamie watching us.

It must have been gone two when we got back home. The house was quiet. Even the cat was asleep. I put on some music and made coffee. That's one of the good things about old stone houses like ours. The walls and ceilings are thick. When you're upstairs, you can't hear anything that's happening downstairs. I lit some candles and turned the lights down low. We sat on the sofa and I kicked off my shoes. Duncan started kissing me. His T-shirt was damp and he smelt deliciously of smoke and alcohol. I took the bobble out of my hair so it was hanging loose, and he ran his fingers through it and caressed my scalp. It was like Indian head massage. Oh, man! If I'd been a cat I would have been purring fit to burst.

We went pretty quickly from sitting side by side, to lying side by side, to lying on top of each other. I was on my back with my head on the sofa armrest. Duncan had rolled on top of me. I put my hands under his clothes and caressed his warm skin. Then I caught hold of the bottom of his shirt and pulled it off over his shoulders so he was bare-chested. It was the first time I'd seen him without a shirt and I was amazed at how muscular he was. Jamie works out at his mum's gym all the time and he's forever flexing his pecs and showing off his six-pack. But Jamie's muscles are cosmetic – like a fashion accessory. Duncan just looked strong. He looked like someone who'd hauled up lobster pots and dragged boats across sand and ridden everywhere on a bike all his life.

I planted a kiss right in the middle of his chest, where there was a little tuft of dark hair. He tasted lovely. We kissed each other harder. His hands were all over me – down my thighs and inside my blouse and across my stomach as far as the waistband of my jeans. I really wanted him. He had his tongue in my mouth, which I took as a cue to go further. I slipped my hands down his stomach and started unbuttoning his fly – but he stopped me, softly catching hold of my hand. He stopped kissing me and propped himself up on his elbows. Then he looked at me for a long time, ruffling my hair with his fingers. I couldn't work out what he was thinking.

"Maybe we should sleep," he said, rolling off me.

Sleep? That was the last thing I wanted to do!

Duncan got up off the sofa and pulled his T-shirt back on over his head. I stood up, rearranged my clothing and blew out the candles.

I wonder now – looking back – if that was the moment things started to go wrong. Was it all my fault for coming on too strong? Was I more in love with him than he was with me? Was I in deeper? Was I making a fool of myself? Or was the plain and simple truth just that he didn't really fancy me – end of story?

I went to bed with an aching, hungry feeling. At the top of the stairs, he kissed me on the cheek. Then he went along the landing to Al's room – "the spare room", as Mum calls it, now that Alice is at university – where Mum had made up a bed for him. I watched his back disappear behind Al's door. Then I went along the passageway to my room and put on my Winnie the Pooh pyjamas.

18

DUNCAN

I've been sitting looking at the sea all afternoon – in the grass above the bay, beside the burial ground. It's a hot day. No wind. Grandpa would have liked to sit out here, surrounded by flowers. He'd have woven a story for me the way the old women on the island weave cloth. It would have been a story about the sea.

Before he got Alzheimer's disease, Grandpa was a great talker. He'd tell me about mermaids and faery folk and fishermen as we walked by the shore. Some of the stories were ancient Rimsay tales, handed down to him from his mother and his grandmother and his great grandmother before that. But some were his own – tales about love and loss and the strange kingdoms under the sea, tales that came spinning from his head like shiny threads.

When he got ill and started drifting far off from us like a boat in the fog, talking shite and asking the same questions over and over again, it was the stories that stayed. Sometimes he'd go for days without any real communication, wandering about, barely recognising us. He'd forget where he was or he'd walk out of the house across the machair and not be able to remember the way back. Sometimes he did dangerous things. He let pans boil dry, or he put washing too near the fire, or he walked too close to the water's edge in the harbour. And he'd forget what had happened two minutes beforehand, so you could tell him something and then it was as if the words had never been spoken – erase and rewind. Then, just for a fleeting moment, he'd be completely all there. It was as if he was out of focus for most of the time and everything was blurred and fuzzy then suddenly he'd come into focus, one hundred percent sharp. For a matter of minutes he'd be like he was before – funny and witty and quick off the mark. And often as not he'd come out with a story – recalling it in perfect detail.

He did that one day last spring, soon after my visit to Manchester. We were sitting on the bench outside our house, facing the shore. It was warm. There were primroses in the grass. He told me my favourite story – the one about the selkie. This is how it goes . . .

Once upon a time, there was a young man who walked along the shore. Quite by chance he happened upon a group of selkies playing on the beach. (Selkies, in case you don't know, are sea faeries that look like seals but can unzip their skins to appear as beautiful humans. Yes, I know it's bollocks, but it's a story isn't it?) The selkies that the young man saw were beautiful young women (of course) with golden hair. ("Like that young lassie of yours," Grandpa said with a twinkle in his eye, which astonished me because when Isabel came to stay with us he acted like she was invisible.) When the selkies saw the young man they grabbed their skins and, putting them back on, they slipped quickly into the sea – all except for one, who was so busy chasing a feather across the sand that she didn't act fast enough. The young man grabbed her discarded seal skin and gripped it tight. Now, this bit's important: sometimes selkies fall in love with humans and go onto land to be with them, but they always end up tiring of the human lover and returning to the sea – and then the human dies of a broken heart. However, if a human holds onto a selkie's skin and refuses to give it back, he can force her to stay forever in the world of mortals. As this selkie was extremely beautiful, the young man decided to hold her captive. So he hid her skin and begged her to marry him – and she did. She lived with him for many years and bore him many children. She was a good wife and a loving mother . . . But she was never fully happy in the human world and she pined for the sea. Then one day, one of her children came upon the hidden skin quite by chance and, dragging the mysterious thing out of its hiding place, he took it to his mother. Seeing her long lost seal skin, the selkie mother seized it with delight, put it on and slid into the sea never to be seen again. End of story.

You see now why I say island people are a little mad? These are the stories I was brought up on.

Maybe that's why things went wrong with Isabel. Our worlds were too different. She was a selkie and I was a boring old human. Or was it the other way round? I was the selkie and I needed to get away – back to the sea. Or did I just balls it up – no excuses?

I knew she was hurt that we didn't go all the way that night in Manchester. She was distant and quiet the next morning. It wasn't that I didn't find her attractive. God, no! It was about commitment. I think right from the start I had this lurking fear that she'd get sick of me; that she'd find someone more exciting, more flashy, more like her. So I held myself back a bit. Avoided getting in too deep. Meet Duncan MacLeod – commitment phobe. Next thing you know I'll be growing my fringe all floppy like Hugh Grant. (Did you see *Four Weddings and a Funeral?* You didn't? Forget it then.)

Not 'doing it' (I hate that phrase) – despite the candlelight and the alarmingly soundproof house and Isabel unbuttoning my jeans – was about other things too. My Catholic upbringing, for example. My moral code. Okay, so no one stays a virgin until they're married any more, not even on Rimsay. But the ideal is still there. That sex is a big deal. That it's about permanence and love.

Am I just old fashioned, or what?

Alright, in the light of what's happened since, I'm a bloody hypocrite. But nobody's perfect are they?

19

MACY

Where would you rather be? The south of France, or Manchester, England? Hard choice, eh? Okay, what would you rather be doing? Lying by the poolside or serving coffee to frazzled shoppers with body odour problems? I was really looking forward to my holiday with the Brights. I'd even bought myself a new bikini. But in view of recent events it seemed wise to cancel. (What Isabel actually said to me was that she never beeping wanted to see me again so I should shove my beeping ticket up my beeping beep! Do you get the picture?)

Since I'm permanently strapped for cash, getting a couple of weeks' work seemed too good an opportunity to miss. What was I thinking of? I used to like this place! I used to like coffee! Isabel and I were regular customers, serious cappuccino drinkers, caffeine mainliners! Now I'm a Starbucks waitress on less than the minimum wage and I'm starting to hate even the *smell* of coffee! And the next person that tells me there isn't enough brown stuff sprinkled on the top can just . . . (I'll let you complete that sentence yourself!) You know that frothing machine – the steam thing that makes the milk foam, that sounds like an elephant sucking on a drinking straw – well, listening to it for ten hours a day starts to scramble your brain. That and the heat. Because guess what? Manchester is having a heat wave. Not just Manchester, either – the whole of the UK. Maybe even the Outer Hebrides! So what's the deal? Is this my punishment or something?

When I get my ten-minute break I dash outside and sit in the square beside the stone tulip, just to get some rays on my face. Okay so it's not the same as being on the beach at Cannes but I guess I should be grateful Isabel didn't poison me. (That won't make sense just yet, but don't worry, it will . . .)

A woman with three bad-tempered kids and too many carrier bags just left the table by the window so I'm clearing it up now – stacking all their detritus onto my tray. Now I get to polish it with my squirty hygiene spray and my dinky little cloth. God, I hate housework! This table is the one Iz and I always used to sit at. I can see our ghosts hovering around it. Look! Do you see them? There we are, all smiley and uncomplicated.

We were such good friends, Izzy and me. Hell, what went wrong? It's not like I didn't say sorry . . .

We came in here the day of the audition. Did she tell you about the audition yet? She didn't. That surprises me. Hey, I'm talking capital letters here. I'm talking about The Audition. The Big One . . .

20

ISABEL

The NYT? National Youth Theatre? Sure, it's a big deal. It's like the difference between playing football or hockey or netball for your school and playing for the England Under Twenty-Ones. It's the best. The cream of the cream.

Doe suggested we audition – Macy and me. (Doe's my super-luscious wonderful right-on lesbian drama teacher – Ms Redman to everyone except the Sixth Form.) She said it would be a life changing experience.

Auditions were in April in Manchester. (Not *just* Manchester, of course, all over the country. But we did *ours* in Manchester, naturally.) We were due there at eleven-ten (me) and eleven-twenty (Macy), so we had to get out of French – which didn't go down too well. (Lots of sighing from Mr Horner.) Actually we skipped English too, because no way was I showing up at an audition in my school clothes and besides I was ill with nerves.

Deciding what to wear proved surprisingly difficult. Should I go as "Ballet Isabel" – serious Performing Arts student: hair scraped back in a bun, accentuated cheek bones, lycra, dancing shoes? Or should I go as "Pop Idol Isabel": messy hair, bare navel, embroidered jeans, lots of beads, glittery eye shadow? Or "Casual Isabel": cord pants, T-shirt, denim jacket, minimal make-up?

"Why don't you just go as 'Laid-back I-Don't-Need-To-Make-An-Effort Isabel' in your purple dressing gown and Scooby Doo slippers?" Macy said. She was standing in front of my mirror wiping lipgloss across her bottom lip. I was still in my underwear. "Either way, Iz, could you just hurry up!" she said.

I put my hair in a scrunchy. Then I changed my mind and took it out again. "Which trousers?" I said, holding up two pairs.

"Those ones?" Macy pointed to my jeans.

"Sure?" I said.

"Sure," said Macy.

"They don't make my bum look too big?"

"Isabel, stop being such a stress head! We're going to miss the bus!" Macy was inching towards the door.

I put my jeans on quick and grabbed a jacket. "Eye make-up or no eye make-up?" I asked. (I hate the way nerves make me so indecisive!)

"Whatever!" said Macy. She was wearing normal stuff. The same as she wears for school. How come she was so unflustered?

On the bus I got a text from Duncan: "*Knock em ded!*"

"Bless!" I said.

Macy pulled a face when I showed her.

Ten minutes isn't very long to make an impression. We had to do two pieces from memory – one from Shakespeare and one from a Twentieth Century play – each lasting two minutes max. I did my Shakespeare piece first – Miranda's first speech from *The Tempest* where she describes watching a shipwreck. I know it inside out. I did it just as in our production, with the same moves and gestures. I imagined waves crashing in front of me – like the waves that pounded Duncan's boat.

There were two people watching – a man and a woman. They sat behind a table and smiled at me and wrote things on my application form, but they gave nothing away. I couldn't tell whether they liked my performance or not.

For my modern piece I chose a speech from *My Mother Said I Never Should* – Jackie's speech from right at the end of the play, where she's telling her daughter Rosie why she gave her away when she was a baby. How she tried to survive as a single parent with no money in a student flat and couldn't manage it. How she loved her really, always had, even though she'd abandoned her. It's a pretty emotional scene. One minute she's angry, the next she's crying. Then she's pleading to be understood. I wanted to sound sympathetic but not pitiful. I imagined Rosie standing in front of me – glowering at me, demanding an explanation. Why had I let her believe her grandma was her mother all these years? Why was I telling her all this stuff now?

At the end of the speech there was a long pause before they spoke, which I took to be a good sign. Then they started asking me questions. What did I think was the value of theatre? Why did I want to perform? What did I think I Isabel Bright could offer to the NYT? I said lots of things about drama being character-building and about teamwork. (Doe's really hot on that. "If one falls down, you all fall down," she keeps saying. "Everyone is vital. There are no stars. This is live theatre, not Hollywood!") And I said that what I loved about performing most was the way, on stage with other people, you kind of make magic together. You create something that's not real but at the same time it's more real than the nose on your face. I'm not sure I actually said that exactly, but I said something like that, and they wrote it down on their piece of paper. Then my ten minutes was up and it was Macy's turn.

We were on a high afterwards. Macy had made them both laugh with her modern speech, and the guy had winked at her as she left the room.

"Won't it be amazing if we both get in!" I said. I gave her a hug.

"London, here we come!" Macy said with a big grin on her face.

Going back to school seemed too much of an anticlimax, so we went to Starbucks instead and celebrated with two White Mocha Cappuccinos Venti – extra large!

21

MACY

We got the letters in May. I rang Isabel as soon as the post arrived. "Have you got mail?" I said.

Isabel's postman comes way later than ours. This was eight twenty-seven a.m. and he still hadn't showed. "Don't tell me! Don't tell me!" she squealed down the phone. "I want to open my letter first." That was typical Isabel. How come *I* had to wait to tell her my good news?

Her mail still hadn't arrived when she left for school. All through French she was unbelievably fidgety. "Go on then. Tell me. Was it good or bad?" she said, at the end of the lesson.

"You said you didn't want to know," I said. I pretended I'd taken the huff but really I was dying to tell her. Anyway, huffs are Isabel's department. I don't do huffs. If I'm pissed with someone then I just say so!

"Are you in or not?" She was looking at me intensely. Isabel-intense.

I faked disappointment so she'd think I'd failed the audition. "Well," I said, "they told us competition was stiff."

"Oh god, Macy! Was it a no?"

I kept her waiting a moment or two longer, made her squirm a little. Then I said, "I got in!" and she screamed and hugged me. We were in the corridor, outside the Textiles room.

"Lezzers!" said a Year Ten boy as he went by.

We walked arm in arm up the stairs to the Sixth Form common room. "If you're in, then I must be too!" Isabel said. How tactful is that? Like I told you, sometimes Isabel speaks before she thinks.

Isabel didn't make it through the morning. The suspense was too much for her. She made up an excuse about not feeling well and took a bus home so she could read her mail. I was in the cafeteria queue when she called me. "OH YES!" she yelled down the phone. "Look out, London!" She was in too. We'd both made it.

We'd got places on the NYT summer acting course. The letter said we'd be based at a school in north London and that we'd be working with fourteen other people, all our age, on a devised production of a Greek play by Euripides.

We were in the local paper: "*Manchester girls have stars in their eyes!*" They took a cheesy photo of Iz and I standing back-to-back beside the school entrance. I sent a copy to Moma Paige and she called me to say she'd stuck it on her refrigerator. Bless!

22

DUNCAN

There was a voicemail message on my phone from Isabel when I came out of my exam – English Literature Paper 2. I'd had my phone switched off all morning. I guess she'd forgotten I had an exam. The message was high pitched and squeaky. "*Answer your phone! Answer your phone! I got good news! I'm in! To the NYT. Yahoo! I'm SOOOOO HAPPY!!!!!!!! Call me!!*"

I was pleased for her, of course. I knew how much it meant. She's really serious about theatre, Isabel is, you see. (I guess you know that already.) She's very focussed about what she wants to do. I envy that in a way. My future is rather more hazy. I'm following my nose. I'll see how things turn out . . .

I'd be lying if I said I wasn't disappointed though. I'd had this idea we might spend the summer together. Or part of it anyway. I really wanted Isabel to come to Rimsay again, when the weather was good. I wanted her to see the wild flowers in the machair and swim in the sea – when it's warm enough not to give you heart failure. I'd even had this idea I could take her out in the boat – out beyond the point just as the tide is turning, where (if you're lucky) – you sometimes see a whole troupe of porpoises jumping. Another time, maybe? Dream on Duncan!

Okay, so she'd rather be in London treading the boards, doing her thing. I can't say I blame her. Rimsay community centre or the Lyric Hammersmith? Hard choice that one!

23

A month in London rehearsing a play. The chance to perform in the West End. Voice classes. Movement classes. Stage-fighting lessons. This was going to be *real* theatre. Like professionals. No coursework to complete. No essays. No French lessons to ask to be excused from. (And no Mr Horner sighing and doing that smoothing thing with his hair that he does when he's irritated!) Just drama twenty-four seven. How cool is that?

But it gets better! Not only did we get to spend four weeks in London, but then (the letter said) there was the possibility of our production transferring to Edinburgh for a spell on the Festival Fringe! That would be two capital cities in one month. And Scotland too – which meant Duncan. All this and true love as well. I couldn't believe my luck!

"I could join you in Edinburgh," he said. We were talking on the phone. I was running a bath full of strawberry bubbles. "Where will you be staying? We could stay at Ned's uncle's house. He lives in Edinburgh. Edinburgh's fantastic. Especially at Festival time. You'll love it." Duncan was gabbling, the way he does when he gets excited about something. Verbal diarrhoea!

I dipped my hand in the mountain of foam. "Or there's Al's place," I said. "Her uni flat will be empty in the holidays. She says Macy and I can stay there, if we don't trash the joint!"

"Great!" Duncan said. I hooked the phone under my chin and started peeling off my socks. "We could try and get a gig – the Posh Porpoises, I mean. Play the fringe too . . ."

"Sure," I said. I turned off the taps. The bathroom was full of steam.

"Hey," said Duncan. "I'll be able to watch your play. See you on stage at last."

I was lowering myself into the bath. I winced at how hot it was.

"I'd better go now," I said. "Unless you want to take a bath with me!"

"There's an offer I can't refuse," Duncan said, laughing.

My handset was getting slippery with the steam. "I need to put the phone down," I said. "Call me back in half an hour."

"What's the play?" he said. I didn't quite catch the question.

"The what?" I said.

"The play," he said again. "What is it?"

"Some Greek thing," I said. "*Medea*?"

24

How much do you know about *Medea*? Not a lot? Okay, I'll tell you the story. But first, a warning: if you're eating your lunch while you're reading this, I suggest you stop. It might make you throw up! So, here we go . . .

There's this guy Jason. (Did you see *Jason and the Argonauts?* Well that's him.) He's the son of Aeson, who *should* be the king except that his half-brother, Pelias, has usurped him. (Sounds a bit like *The Tempest*, huh?) So Jason is on the run, living in exile. But then he decides to go back home and claim his inheritance. Now, Pelias (the uncle) is suspicious of Jason (something about him only wearing one sandal, but I'll spare you the details) so he sets Jason a supposedly impossible task. He tells him he has to sail to some place or other and fetch the Golden Fleece. (Are you keeping up? That's just the background info.)

So off goes Jason with a bunch of mates in a ship called the Argo, and he has a load of adventures with dragons and clashing rocks and all that jazz. And to cut a long story short, he meets Medea. Now, Medea is the daughter of the king of the place with the Golden Fleece in it – and she's a bit of a looker. She also has magic powers which she uses to help Jason – having, as in all good stories, fallen in love with him. It's because of her that Jason manages to outwit the king and get the Golden Fleece. (That's important! She's saved his bacon. He really should be grateful to her.)

Having *got* the Golden Fleece Jason scarpers – taking the lovely Medea with him, and her brother goes too. (Don't ask me why!) But just as they're trying to escape, Medea's father catches up with them. So Medea murders her brother, cuts him up into little bits and throws him into the sea – just to give her father something else to worry about. Like a decoy. (Scary lady, huh? She's so madly in love that she murders her own brother to help Jason escape. This is serious passion. We're talking Greek tragedy here.)

Having killed her brother, Medea then engineers the murder of Pelias (Jason's uncle) too – so that Jason can go back home and be the prince, like he's meant to be. So off they go to Iolchus, Jason's home city, which seems fair enough since Medea (not surprisingly, in the light of her dismembered kid brother) isn't welcome at home any more. Jason marries Medea and they have two sons. But things don't work out in Iolchus, so pretty soon they're exiled to Corinth.

Now if Jason had any sense, at this point he'd just keep his head down. Get a steady job. Mow the lawn. Play baseball with the kids. Go for a night out with the lads from time to time, maybe. But stay out of trouble.

But no. He has an affair. He gets involved with the daughter of the King of Corinth (what is it with men and princesses?) and he *leaves* Medea. Bad move. This is a woman who's already been responsible for *two* murders. She's not exactly what you'd call mentally stable. You're a stupid guy, Jason. You should have kept your zipper tight shut.

So, like I said, Jason goes off, leaving Medea with the two kids. Then he says he wants to marry Little Miss Corinth, so Medea rants and raves. (Well, wouldn't you?) So Creon, that's the King of Corinth (father to Jason's new gal) says Medea's dangerous and he'll have to exile her. But where can she go? She's already had to flee her homeland *and* been kicked out of Iolchus. She's a displaced person. We're talking asylum seeker here. We're talking desperate.

So Medea pleads with the king. She asks him to let her stay one more day and – soft touch that he is – he agrees.

Now she sets about a revenge plan that will make your toes curl. We're not talking wronged-wife-cutting-the-sleeves-out-of-his-jackets here. We're not even talking pet-rabbit-stewed-in-the-pot. (Did you see *Fatal Attraction?*) No, this is heavy duty revenge. This is certificate eighteen.

Step One: Medea pretends she's really happy for

Jason. The princess is a really nice girl. Marrying her makes a lot of sense. Medea wishes them well. She really does. She has no hard feelings. Being married to Jason, even for a short time, was great. He made her prosperous. He made her famous. He gave her two great kids. All good things come to an end . . . etc. etc. Sucker that he is, Jason falls for it.

Step two: Medea sends a present to Jason's new bride: a pretty dress and a sparkly gold crown. Just a little something to show she wishes them well. A gift for the happy couple. She gets her two little sons to deliver the present to the palace – and they're *so cute*, how could the princess refuse them anything? The only snag is: the dress and crown are laced with lethal poison and when the princess puts them on she burns alive. Nasty!

Step three: Just in case Jason is still in doubt as to how Medea feels . . . just in case he hasn't grasped that she is SERIOUSLY PISSED OFF WITH HIM . . . she murders their children. No fancy tricks. No poison. She just runs them through with a sword while they scream for mercy.

And that's where the story ends. Now, Jason – do you get the picture? Do you wish you'd kept your trousers on?

It's a little over the top, you have to admit, but then, when did the Ancient Greeks ever do anything by half measures?

25

DUNCAN

I went and read *Medea* as soon as I knew that was Isabel's play. There was a copy of it in the school library. It's pretty grim, don't you think? Euripides wrote it in four hundred BC so it's ancient too, although it seems incredibly modern. Sexual jealousy – and the crimes it drives people to – is a fairly timeless theme, I suppose. Nothing changes. Girl plus boy plus another girl (or boy) equals trouble. The eternal triangle. It's everywhere. Take *Othello* for example. He's so convinced that his wife, Desdemona, is having it away with Iago that he murders her by putting a pillow over her face. Then there's Leontes in *The Winter's Tale* who ties himself in knots imagining Hermione is having an affair with his friend Polixenes, and has her locked up in prison to punish her.

I was reading the *Decameron* the other day, which is a collection of bawdy Italian stories from the thirteen hundreds. My English teacher says they influenced Chaucer's *Canterbury Tales* – most of which are filthy too! (Okay, so I'm reading a lot this summer. That's because I got my university reading list. And let's face it, I haven't got much else to do . . .)

Anyway there's this very raunchy tale. I suppose you want to hear it, don't you? Here's a synopsis: Two men are friends, then one of them sleeps with the other's wife. The wronged husband finds out and locks the lover (his friend) in a trunk. Then he has sex on top of the locked trunk with the lover's wife. End of story. So what's that meant to prove?

One of the books on my list is *The Age of Innocence* by Edith Wharton. I noticed there was a movie of it in the video shop, so I watched it. Guess what? It's about love triangles too. This bloke called Newland Archer (Daniel Day Lewis) is all set to marry his nice fiancée, May Welland (Wynona Ryder). Then he meets Countess Olenska (Michelle Pfeiffer) and falls for her in a big way. He spends the rest of the movie going mad with suppressed passion until it all gets too much for him and he meets Ms Pfeiffer in a cabin in the woods. It's all very buttoned down and Victorian – lots of lace gloves and corsets and complicated clothing, and nobody actually getting their kit off. It was a bit slow for my taste. Michelle Pfeiffer was pretty nice though. She looks a bit like Isabel, don't you think?

Okay, so everything comes back to Isabel . . . Well, like I was saying, I read *Medea*. And looking back now, don't you think it's a bit ironic that *that* was the play they were doing this summer?

26

ISABEL

I'm sitting in a square in the middle of a French village, drinking Orangina and eating a nectarine. I'm under one of those big white cotton parasols, because it's so hot. There's a brown-and-white dog lying under the table – no owner in sight. It's wearing a red cotton bandana around its neck instead of a collar, which seems to be the fashion with French dogs. I move my foot away from its dribbling mouth and it turns and looks at me as if I've offended it. Soz!

I'm thinking about child murderers, which you might find a bit odd, in the circumstances. Except that I just saw the front of a French newspaper. There was this missing children case going on just before we left England, see. Two little girls – sisters, both blonde and gorgeous – disappear on a summer's day. The last anyone sees of them, they're playing with a ball in a barley field beside their house. Everyone thinks they've been abducted. Their mother – a single parent with big black rings under her eyes – goes on TV and makes a tearful appeal to their supposed kidnapper.

There was a search going on the day we came to France. I saw footage of policemen with dogs on a telly in the cafeteria on the cross-channel ferry.

But just now, when I went into the tabac to buy my drink, I saw a headline that said *"Monstre Mère!"* (Monster Mother!) My French isn't great but it's good enough to get the basic gist of a story. It seems they've arrested the girls' mother on suspicion of murder.

The paper said an angry mob of protesters threw rocks at the police van as they took the woman away. I'm not sure I'd do *that*. I wouldn't stand outside her house with a placcard and hurl abuse at her, like people do with paedophiles. But I do have difficulty understanding how any woman can murder her kids. That was a bit of a problem for me with *Medea*. I mean, poisoning your husband's lover is one thing, isn't it? But killing your own children? I don't think so. You can't justify that, however much you've been hurt.

Duncan put me on to a version of the *Medea* story written by a Scottish feminist poet. I bought it at the National Theatre bookshop while we were in London. There was some subtle differences to the original script. Like in this version, the murder of the kids is downplayed a bit and the playwright doesn't have the children screaming and begging their mother for mercy the way Euripides does. Plus Medea makes this great long speech before she kills her kids about how she really loves them, but this is the only way; and she makes out that by killing them she's saving the children from the savage revenge of their enemies after she is exiled. It's like: *I'm doing this for your own good.*

It'll hurt me more than it hurts you. I suppose that makes it a bit more palatable. But it's still vile!

We had a big argument about child murder – infanticide I think it's called, isn't it? – the day we first read through the play in London. We were in a pub on Euston Road. Macy was talking about some programme she'd seen on TV about a woman with post-natal depression who murdered her baby. She got a three-year prison sentence, but all that time they had to keep her locked up in the jail for fear the other prisoners would attack her. Macy was arguing that the woman didn't know what she was doing and shouldn't have got a prison sentence at all. Leon, this guy from Liverpool, started talking about Myra Hindley – that woman who tortured kids (other people's, not her own) and did thirty-five years in jail. He was going on about how they could never have let her out because half the population were ready to lynch her.

"It's the ultimate crime, isn't it – murdering kids?" this girl called Charlotte said. She was chain-smoking roll-ups and blowing out plumes of smoke all over the rest of us. "And murdering *your own* kids," she said, "well, that's unforgivable, isn't it?"

"Nothing's unforgivable," I said, swigging down my half pint of orange juice.

What was it Duncan had said? *"Forgiveness is as vital as air . . ."*

Nothing is unforgivable. What did *I* know about it?

27

MACY

Isabel was miscast in my opinion. I mean, don't get me wrong, I think she's very talented. As Miranda in *The Tempest* she was perfect. She does innocence, tenderness, falling in love – all those romantic leading lady things – really well. And she was good in *My Mother Said* . . . She can do Victims and Women-Who've-Been-Misunderstood and Tantrums and Family Arguments. But dark passion, screaming jealousy, blood-curdling revenge? That's not really Isabel Bright, is it? I mean, *you've* met her . . . would *you* cast her as Medea?

There were sixteen of us in the group – ten girls, six boys. For once the gender imbalance didn't really matter, because in *Medea* there's a whole chorus of Corinthian women who get to tell the story and comment on what Medea's doing and try to stop her chopping up the kids.

The play wasn't cast right away. For the first three days we just did a bunch of workshop stuff – voice classes and movement and role-plays and daft games. We were based in a school in Camden. Our director was this crazy guy with a booming voice called Patrick O'Shane. He was mental. I guess he was watching us, sussing us out. He told us who was who on the Thursday morning. We were all sat round sweating, sipping at our water bottles after a fiendish warm-up. (I'd lost four pounds in the first three days from all the exercise!)

Casting the boys' parts was easy. Leon, this rather tasty guy from Liverpool (more of him later!), was Jason. A guy called Sean was Creon, the King of Corinth. King Aegeus of Athens was a weird guy called Jonty, who looked like Rowan Atkinson. Ben from Birmingham was Medea's children's tutor. Dan-with-the-Tan (as we nicknamed him) was a messenger. And a skinny bloke called Simon was one of the sons.

I thought Charlotte would be Medea. She was really tall and wore black goth clothes and she had a sort of manic edge to her – like you wouldn't want to get on the wrong side of her. She'd have brought a certain sinister energy to it – in my opinion. If I'd been directing the play, she would have been my choice. In the end, Patrick gave her the part of Medea's nurse. *Isabel* was Medea, and the rest of us were the Chorus of women – apart from a tiny girl called Louise who looked like a pixie, who was Medea's other son.

So there we were, cast assembled. Ready to take the West End by storm. Did you ever see the movie of *Fame?* It's very early Eighties – very headbands and leg-warmers. It's about a bunch of stage school students in New York, and they keep breaking into these amazing song-and-dance routines. There's this black guy called Leroy who starts off with an attitude problem, almost quits the course – but then, in the nick of time, gets his act together. Very Hollywood! Anyway, there's this scene when they all spill out of the college into the street doing this musical number and Leroy breakdances on the roof of a taxi. It's cool. A little cheesy perhaps. But cool. Well I'd kind of pictured the NYT would be like that. You know, that we'd be tap dancing round Trafalgar Square and bursting into song in front of Buckingham Palace. That we'd all be FAMOUS! Well, call me sentimental . . .

28

I think Macy was a little miffed she didn't get a bigger part in the play. She was a little off with me when Patrick read out the cast list.

I was *thrilled* to be Medea. Well, it was a huge challenge – to get inside the head of the character and, you know, understand her motives. Find out what makes her tick. To be honest, when we first read through the play I thought Medea's revenge was way over the top. I mean, okay so Jason's been a scumbag. I can understand her feeling angry. I can understand her wanting revenge, even. But poisoning? It's a bit extreme, don't you think?

The scene where the princess gets poisoned is really disgusting. You don't get to actually see it (thank god!) but it's described pretty graphically. This messenger (Dan-with-the-Tan) comes on to the stage and tells Medea what's happened. It's not just Jason's lover who's died, but her father Creon, too – poisoned by touching her corpse. Medea wants all the gory details. *"Tell me, how did they die?"* she asks. *"You'll give me double pleasure if their death was horrible."* So he tells her. And it's horrible alright.

He describes how the princess took the crown and,

looking in the mirror, arranged it on top of her hair. And how she put on the embroidered gown and twirled about in it. Then the sudden change of colour in her face, the staggering about and twitching limbs; how she started to froth and foam at the mouth and her eyes rolled back in her head. How the old woman watching her realised what was happening and let out a terrible howl. And how a maid ran to fetch the king. How the princess's head seemed to catch fire under the poisoned coronet and the dress seemed to be devouring her. How blood dripped from her head, and her body was so contorted and disfigured that she looked unrecognisable in a matter of minutes. How her flesh seemed to drip off her bones like gum oozing from a pine tree until she fell down dead. And how Creon (the king), bursting into the room and throwing himself on her body to weep, appeared to stick fast to her like ivy on a laurel branch.

Sick, or what?

"That was so gross," I said. We were taking a break in the sun. I was lying on a wall with my knees pointing up to the sky. Leon had just offered me a swig of his Coke. Macy was singing *Summertime*.

"It's a great speech," said Dan-with-the-Tan. "I'm going to really make a meal of it. Do it like a slasher movie – all that bubbling blood and oozing foam . . ." He pulled a grotesque face and laughed like a pantomime villain.

"Wouldn't it be more fun if we actually saw it happen?" said Charlotte, stubbing out her cigarette on the wall.

"I don't think the budget runs to special effects," Leon said, "sadly."

"Okay, folks. Time!" said Patrick, poking his head out of the studio door.

We went back inside. He got us to do an improvisation about revenge, in threes. I was with Leon and Charlotte.

"Okay, listen up," said Patrick, "One of you is A, one is B, one is C. A and B – you've fallen out. You're having an argument. A has done something to hurt B. *You* decide what the issues are – but make it something serious. That's the first part. Second part: B tells C how he or she is feeling and you plan an act of revenge – I'll leave the details to your imagination." Patrick looked around at us and there was a ripple of sadistic laughter. "Third part: A and B again," he said. "Show us the revenge and how things pan out. I want real emotions. Convincing dialogue. Believable characters. No playing for laughs. Does that make sense? Shall I just re-cap? . . ."

Our scenario went like this. Leon was Charlotte's brother. He'd taken her kids out for the day to a theme park, for a treat. On the way back he'd crashed the car. One of Charlotte's kids was horribly injured

– facially disfigured. Leon was breathalised and found to be over the limit. Charlotte was understandably angry. I was Leon's girlfriend. I started out defending him but Charlotte shot me down in flames. He was irresponsible. He was a jerk. It was just like him to put his own desire for a drink before the safety of her kids. How would *he* feel if he had a mangled face? If he had to spend the rest of his life being stared at – being thought hideous, like the elephant man. She told me she'd make him pay. And what did she do? She attacked him with a hot iron while he was sleeping. I had to make an imaginary phone call describing his burnt face to an ambulance crew . . .

"That was frighteningly authentic, Charlotte," Patrick said. "Just remind me not to fall asleep anywhere near *you!*"

After we'd watched all five scenarios – five grisly episodes of vengeance – we took another break and went for coffee.

"To tell you the truth, I have a problem with the whole revenge thing," I said to Macy. I said it quietly in case people thought I was a wimp. "I mean, two wrongs don't make a right, do they? An eye for an eye and a tooth for a tooth – isn't it healthier to let things lie? I mean, revenge is so *destructive* . . ."

"Isabel, you're just too *nice*," said Macy, with a slightly patronising smile. Leon was leaning across the table, fiddling with the sugar sachets. Macy was trying to impress him by putting me down. I hate it when people do that. I must have looked a bit hurt because Macy back-tracked a little.

"Yeah, maybe you're right," she said. "Revenge is pointless. But let's face it, if Medea just laid down and took the shit, it would make a real boring play!"

I laughed.

"Anyway," she said. "Medea's not sweet like you."

Sweet? Why did she think I was sweet? Maybe I *was* sweet, back then . . . One thing is certain. The way I felt about Medea in July, and the way I feel about her now, aren't the same. Now, I know a little of what she feels like. I know how cheated and cheap she feels. And I know how betrayal does poison things – how it's like a deadly toxin trickling down, contaminating everything it touches.

29

DUNCAN

I liked the sound of Edinburgh. Well, who wouldn't? The Festival is wicked. I went once before, with Ned. We stayed with his uncle. It was buzzing. There were all these mime artists and jugglers in the street, and people dressed-up giving out handbills for plays all up and down the Royal Mile, and gigs and shows in every pub, and crowds and crowds of people. *O brave new world . . .*

Ned tried to get the Posh Porpoises a gig. We hit the fringe website and filled in a registration form, and then they sent us all this bumpf about how to get a venue and everything.

"It's going to cost us five hundred pounds," he said, a note of despair in his voice. We were sitting on the pier at Seabay, eating chips, watching the ferry arrive from Oban. "At least."

"How come?" I said. I was short of cash – as usual. The weekend in Glasgow with Isabel had cleaned me out and I was still paying Mum back the hundred quid she'd lent me to buy a new guitar amp.

"Shouldn't they be paying *us*?" said Angus, our bass player. "I mean, we're quality, we are! You don't see Liam Gallagher paying for his own gigs, do you?"

Ned was scribbling on the piece of paper his chips were wrapped in, working out the sums, while I looked out across the blue-grey sea. "It's two hundred and fifty quid – plus VAT to be an official Fringe act. Then another hundred at least to hire a venue, plus publicity costs, plus getting there, plus finding somewhere to stay, etc etc."

"Shit!" said Angus. "That's a bit steep. Can't we just turn up and busk in the street? You know, play in the gutter and hope that some A&R man comes along and discovers us!" He laughed, and stuffed a chip into his mouth.

"We'd have to play to at least a hundred people and they'd all have to pay a fiver a head," said Ned, doodling with his pencil.

"So?" Angus said. "We played to two hundred at the New Year's bash."

"Yes," I said, "but on Rimsay there's no competition. In Edinburgh there are millions of acts and gigs and plays, and everyone's trying to drum up an audience. We'd never find a hundred people who'd come and hear a band they hadn't heart of – brilliant as we are!"

"Maybe next year," Ned said. He ate his last chip, scrumpled up the paper and tossed it in the air like a ball. "We can start saving up for it now . . ."

"Sod them!" said Angus, throwing a piece of batter into the sea. A crowd of seagulls swooped from nowhere and one of them caught it before it hit the water. "Edinburgh's pants, anyway," he said. "Who wants to go to a place full of tourists and mime artists?"

"Well, actually *I* do," I said. I licked salt off my fingers.

"Yeah but you just want to get your end away with your English girlfriend," said Angus, smirking at me.

I threw a handful of chips at him but they missed and a dozen seagulls mobbed him instead. It was like that bit with the starlings in Hitchcock's *The Birds*. Did you see that movie? It's a classic.

So, a performance by the Posh Porpoises was a non-starter. But who cared? I was going to have a great time in Edinburgh anyway. Isabel's play was running for four nights. And the rest of the time? Well, we'd be together, wouldn't we? Iz said her sister's flat was empty and we could stay there. She said it might be a bit crowded. Did I mind that? That we'd all be kipping on the floor. There'd be a few of us. Some of the play cast: a bloke called Leon ("You'll like him, he's funny"), and this girl called Charlotte she'd mentioned a lot, and of course, Macy (Ruby Wax meets Bjork). Isabel had talked about Macy so much I felt I knew her already. And I'd seen the photos . . .

30

MACY

Let me tell you about Leon. Oh boy! Where shall I start? Well, he's got gorgeous skin. His dad's Indian and his mum's white, so he's a fantastic sort of coffee colour – cappuccino, in fact. (Okay, so I thought that when I still liked coffee!) And he's got thick black wavy hair and big, big eyes and a pierced eyebrow and beautiful hands. (So I have this thing about guys' hands – what's so weird about that?) Let's say his dress sense is a little unusual. He wears old man jackets from charity shops, and torn shirts, and shoes that look like he's just walked off the set of a Fred Astaire movie – but I like that. It's original. And anyway, he's the sort of guy who would look fabulous in a garbage sack! What else? Well, he's funny and he's clever and he's a great actor. If I'd been Medea and he was Jason, I'd have forgiven him anything.

So, I had a major crush on him while we were in London – like that wasn't obvious! But guess what? He fancied Isabel. Wouldn't you just know it? What *is* it with her?

So there we were, walking through Camden market after a hard day's rehearsing. We'd been doing the scene where Medea and Jason argue spectacularly. Patrick had had this zany idea that those of us in the Chorus should melt into the background when we weren't speaking and become items of furniture – kind of like, walls-have-ears sort of thing. So this girl called Rhia and me we were stood with our hands clasped together to make a chair that Isabel could sit on, and then we moved and became a picture frame at the side of the stage. (What's the problem, can't they afford scenery or something?) Well, Isabel and Leon were shouting at each other and sparks were flying round the rehearsal room and, I tell you, the air was crackling with sexual tension. (Like he'd have left *her* for some soppy Greek princess? I don't think so!)

So there we were, weaving our way between the market stalls, and Isabel stopped to buy a bag of oranges. (She's such a health freak! What's wrong with eating junk food like the rest of us?) We had a free evening and some of the cast were cooking up a plan to meet up for a drink. The trouble was, we were living all over London, and London's a big place, so meeting up after hours was kind of complicated. For example, Isabel and I were staying at Isabel's mum's cousin's house which is in Islington (Northern Line to the Angel). Whereas Charlotte was south of the river near the Elephant and Castle (change at Euston then Bakerloo Line south from Charing Cross). And

Leon – well, he was in a hostel near Oxford Circus (Victoria Line from King's Cross, or Northern Line to Bank then west on the Central Line, or Northern Line west then south to Tottenham Court Road, or catch a Number 19 bus out west!). Like I say, it was complicated.

Isabel was making excuses about wanting to get an early night and needing to learn lines. I knew that what she really wanted was to get home and get on the phone to Duncan, like she did every other night. But Leon was really buttering her up, saying she looked great on four hours sleep a night and she knew all her lines already – which she did. I could see she was flattered. How could she not have been, with Leon coming on to her like that? She's a stronger woman than I am. She turned down the offer of a night with Leon from Liverpool!

"She's attached," I said. Isabel was in a store buying a bottle of Evian.

"So?" said Leon, as though that had never stopped him before.

"So she's dating someone," I said, stating the obvious. "She's not available. Unlike me." Okay, so that was a terrible chat-up line and I can't quite believe I said it, but four weeks of role-play and trust exercises and you come out with all kinds of trash!

So Leon and I went out for a drink and Isabel

stayed home. And what did we spend the entire evening talking about? Yes, you guessed it! Isabel Bright . . .

"So you two go to school together?"

"Yep."

"In Manchester."

"Yep."

"And she's in your drama group?"

"Yep."

"She's a great actress."

"Yep."

"And she's gorgeous."

"Yep."

"So this guy she goes out with? Is it serious?"

I said it was. I said that they were practically married. And I said Duncan was six foot seven and a body builder . . . and black. So, I lied. I was hoping to put him off her a bit. Make Leon think that Duncan would show up and break his legs if he so much as looked at Isabel again. Well, call me desperate, but it was worth a try!

31

ISABEL

Our apartment is in a sort of holiday village. There's a shared pool – which you've seen already – a shop, a burger bar, a kids play area, etc. And then there's this sandy arena where all the men get together every afternoon and play *boules*. Right beside that there's a row of table-tennis tables, outside in the sun. I was playing there with Pete, my stepdad, today. He was trying to teach me how to put spin on the ball. We were keeping the score in French and every time I did something half-decent (which wasn't very often) Pete shouted *"Bon jouer!"* It was roasting hot and Pete kept fanning himself with the bat and saying, "Mon dieu! Il fait chaud!" We played three games – all of which I lost – and then Pete went off to get the barbecue going on our terrace.

I sat in the shade, under a big tree with flaking bark like camouflage. And I started thinking about Duncan. It must have been the table-tennis. I remembered him in the community hall on Rimsay, playing against Ned. Him pratting about with his long gangling legs. Me sat on the window sill, freezing, in his big grey jumper. Thinking about Duncan's jumper made me suddenly remember the smell of him – salt and outdoors and Lynx "Africa" – and then I thought of his goofy smile, looking at me. For a brief mad moment I really missed him. In fact, I almost sent him a text. Then I pulled myself together and went to help Pete with the charcoal briquettes.

I haven't spoken to Duncan, or texted him, or e-mailed him, in ten days – which is the longest silence *ever* since we first started talking to each other. He's tried texting me a few times since he left, but I just hit delete. It was predictable stuff: "*Sorry!*" Sad face icon. "*Forgive me?*" just like Jamie all over again.

When I was in London I used to text him dozens of times a day. I'd text him when I was sitting on the grass outside the rehearsal rooms during breaks; and when I was on the tube late at night; and when I was at mum's cousin Mark's place, waiting for Macy to hurry up in the shower; and when I was on the top deck of a bus going through Trafalgar Square, or Piccadilly Circus, or up Park Lane; and when I was walking along the South Bank looking at the Houses of Parliament and the London Eye, with skateboarders hurtling by me.

I love London. It's such a happening place. And it all felt so familiar – even though I'd only been a couple of times before. I kept recognising places from the telly and from movies . . . and from Monopoly!

One day I phoned Mum and Pete from a bus stop. "I'm on Bond Street!" I shouted above the noise of the traffic.

"That's my property," shouted Pete, "with a hotel – that's fourteen hundred pounds!"

Another time Mum rang me to ask if everything was okay, and I was on the Old Kent Road near where Charlotte was staying. "Quick, buy some houses," Mum said, "They're cheap down there!" (As you can see, we play a lot of Monopoly in the Bright household.)

Where was I? London, right. No, actually I don't want to talk about Duncan. I want to talk about London, Okay! Doing the play and rehearsing it, and the whole theatrical thing was fantastic, but just being in London was brilliant too. Like, one Sunday afternoon we all went to Kensington Gardens and had a big picnic and played rounders, and then Leon jumped in the Serpentine in his clothes. And we went shopping down the King's Road and I tried on a pair of shoes that cost five hundred pounds. "One day," I said.

"When you're a Hollywood star," said Macy.

"Then you can have six pairs!" said Charlotte.

Macy and I queued for tickets to see Glenn Close at the National Theatre, and we got some returns about two minutes before curtain up.

"God! *Glenn Close*," said Macy as she squeezed into

her seat. "She's such an icon. Did you see *Dangerous Liaisons*? She's so good in that."

"I saw her in *Fatal Attraction*," I said.

"Lock up your bunnies!" said Macy. The man in front turned round and gave us a dirty look and Macy silently flicked him the finger.

Another time, we were on the tube travelling home together – a bunch of us. "Isn't London just the best place?" I said. "I mean it's got everything."

"*He who is tired of London is tired of life!*" said Leon.

"Who said that?" I said.

"I just did," Leon said, winking at me.

I laughed. "No," I said, "isn't it a famous quote from somewhere?"

"Yeah," Leon said. "I just said it, and *I'm* famous!"

"Like, yeah!" said Macy.

Macy started saying she liked New York better than London. "It's more stylish," she said. "More architecturally harmonious." She was trying to impress Leon because she thinks he's clever. Actually he's just a bit of a poser, in my opinion. And he dresses like a loser.

"You're more likely to get shot in New York," I said.

"Not necessarily," said Macy. She narrowed her eyes and leaned forward to whisper, "That guy at the end of the carriage looks pretty dodgy. And what's he got in his sports bag?"

"Sports gear?" said Charlotte, with a *Whatever?* face.

Macy had spooked me. I kept watching the guy's bag, just in case. Then everyone started telling "the night I thought I was going to be attacked" stories – most of which were probably bullshit but, all the same, I was glad when we got back home. That's the one thing I don't like about cities. You don't always feel safe.

But don't get me wrong . . . I really loved London. And I loved Edinburgh too. Or rather, I would have done – if Macy hadn't spoilt it for me.

32

DUNCAN

Isabel's play started on a Wednesday. I couldn't afford to fly over so I caught the ferry to Oban and then took a four-hour train ride to Edinburgh. It was late afternoon when I arrived. I walked across the bridge from Waverley onto Princes Street and caught a bus to Alice's flat, which is down the Dalkeith Road. Isabel was in the bath when I arrived. An Asian guy in an old coat answered the door.

"I'm Duncan," I said. He looked a bit puzzled. "Isabel's boyfriend," I said, helpfully.

"I thought you were black," he said, standing aside to let me in. (Don't ask me what he meant by *that!*) Someone was cooking. The kitchen was full of steam. A girl in black eye-liner went by in her underwear.

"Are you Macy?" I asked.

"No, I'm Charlotte," she said. "Did you want Macy?" Without waiting for me to answer she yelled up the stairs, "MACY! Some guy to see you!"

Macy ran downstairs alarmingly quickly, drying her hair with a towel and looked at me a little blankly. "Hello?" she said, trying to figure out who I was. Then she realised.

"God!" she said. "It's Duncan, isn't it? I didn't

recognise you. No beard!" She stroked her chin and pointed at my face. "I'll tell Isabel," she said. "She's in the bathroom."

Macy ran back upstairs and I heard her banging on the door. "Duncan's here!" she shouted.

"What?" Isabel yelled above the sound of rushing water. "He's early!"

"No! He's on time. *You're* late!" Macy bellowed.

"What time is it?"

I heard the bolt slide across and the door swing open.

"Five thirty," Macy said, more quietly.

"Shit!" I heard Isabel say in a stage whisper . . .

"She won't be long," Macy said, coming back downstairs. "Make yourself at home. Do you want coffee?"

Isabel looked different when she finally came downstairs. She looked tanned for a start, but then I'd only ever seen her in winter before. She had freckles all over her nose and she looked thinner – less cuddly. (Maybe I'd just remembered her wrong.) Her hair was different too. It was sort of curly.

• "Like the hair," I said. I wasn't sure I did but I was breaking the ice, making conversation.

Isabel laughed. "It's for the play," she said. "Heated rollers!" She ran her hand through her fringe. "It makes it easier to put up."

I wasn't sure what she meant by "put up" but then

hair's not really my area of speciality. I kissed her – just a peck on the cheek. All around the room I was aware of people watching us, like I was being sized-up and scrutinized. I would have liked to say hello somewhere a little more private but, what the hell, it was great to see her.

We ate some pasta that Charlotte had cooked and then we got a bus back into the city centre to the venue where they were doing *Medea*. It was an old church hall just off South Clerk Street. There was a poster on the railings outside with a photo of Isabel looking scary in bright red lipstick. *"No one does raw energy better than the NYT. The Scotsman,"* the shoutline said.

Isabel had to be there a whole hour before the performance started, so I had time to kill. I took a walk down the Royal Mile. It was just how I'd remembered the Festival from before, only if anything even busier. There were *so* many people, and theatre posters everywhere and fire-swallowers and a guy on stilts with a hat like an enormous chicken. I felt like I'd just walked onto the set of *Moulin Rouge*.

The play was really good. Vile and depressing, admittedly; but a brilliant production and, like the poster said, full of raw energy. Isabel was extremely good. Even better than I was expecting, in fact. She had stage presence by the bucketload and as for the little black number she was wearing – well, this was a whole new side to Isabel Bright!

After the show we went to a pub and I drank too much lager. Isabel was a little distracted, and there were crowds of people round her telling her how well she'd done and how marvellous she was and how slick it had been for a first night's performance. I should have felt proud, shouldn't I? I *did* feel proud. But I felt a little overlooked as well.

It was only later that I finally got her to myself – and even then, I felt like I was prising her away from the group, like pulling a limpet off a rock or something. We went for a walk up Arthur's Seat, which is this whopping great hill in the middle of Edinburgh. Alright, so it was probably a mad place to go at that time of night after a few too many beers, but I wanted privacy.

It was pretty late by the time we reached the slippy, scrambly bit near the top. We were groping our way in the dark and giggling a lot. Isabel kept tripping and I had to hold on to her so she wouldn't fall. (Well, that was my excuse anyhow!) At the summit there's a big compass and a map showing you what you can see in every direction – except, by then, we couldn't see much at all. Only the stars, and each other. Isabel wanted to work out which way Rimsay was and which way was Manchester. To be honest, I wasn't very interested. I just wanted to kiss her.

I thought it was mutual.

33

MACY

Isabel likes to be a diva. You know, she likes the whole prima donna, private dressing room, leading lady thing. She takes her performances *very* seriously. I mean, don't get me wrong – we were *all* serious about the play. If we hadn't been, we wouldn't have auditioned for the NYT. I mean, who wants to roll around all day on a studio floor being a chair if they don't love the theatre? Who wants to do excruciating warm-up exercises to get strong stomach muscles and improve their diaphragmatic breathing (when they could be lying outside in the sun) if they don't take acting seriously? But Isabel was in a different league from the rest of us – which presumably is why Patrick cast her in the title role.

Isabel started her preparation for the performance with about four hours to go. First she took a long bath to get in the right frame of mind – which was kind of inconvenient when there were eight of us in the one house. I mean, where *were* we supposed to go and pee? Then she put her hair in heated rollers and painted her toe and finger nails bright red and sat stretching in a towel on the bedroom floor with her eyes shut, looking kind of spaced-out and yogic.

If I tried to talk to her, she snapped at me and said she needed space in her head. Yeah, right, Isabel. How much space do you need?

Honestly, I'm not knocking her. I'm sure her attention to detail and the thoroughness of her pre-show preparation was the reason her performances were so damned good. But it was a bit tight on poor Duncan.

I mean, the guy had travelled in from Outer Space to spend time with Isabel, and there he was spending most of his visit mooching around the flat, listening to the distant splash of bath water. She could at least have let him take a bath *with* her!

I did my best to entertain him and keep him company which, in the circumstances, was the least I could do. You could say we were "thrown together" by the absence of Isabel, but I agree that would be a little over-the-top. We watched TV a lot. We watched *Ready Steady Cook* and *Bargain Hunt* and all those ancient black-and-white movies they show in the afternoons. And we chatted. Just chatted.

I'd always said – right from the start when Isabel was giving it the "there's-nothing-going-on, I'm-only-writing-to-him-out-of-pity" treatment – that Duncan seemed a nice guy. That he seemed funny and kind and interesting. And I was right. He's great. We laughed a lot. He's quirky and witty. He likes Eddie Izzard and Billy Conolly and Monty Python and *Smack the Pony* and all the same stuff that I find funny. And, hell, here is a guy that has watched almost as many movies in his lifetime as I have. I suppose on an island there isn't much else to do. He says his English teacher's got shelf-loads of videos – practically every quality movie made in the last twenty years and a load of turkeys besides! – and he just goes round and borrows them.

We were making toast in the ad break halfway through *Pet Rescue*. Duncan was listing his top ten movies of all time.

"*Casablanca*'s gotta to be up there," I said, taking the lid off the peanut butter.

"No," he said. "*Casablanca*'s overrated. Everyone chooses it. *The African Queen* is a better Bogart movie; but it's not in my top ten." He caught my toast as it popped out of the toaster and tossed it to me with a flick of his wrist.

"Olé!" I said, catching it.

"*One Flew Over The Cuckoo's Nest*, definitely," Duncan said, "and *The English Patient*—"

"Not *The English Patient*!" I said. "It's so implausible! And Kristin Scott Thomas – she's weird looking!" I waved my knife at him and he grinned like a split watermelon.

121

"But it's got Juliette Binoche in it," he said, "and the camera work is stunning."

"Yeah," I said, spreading my toast. "I'll give you that."

Duncan listed *Speed* and *The Matrix* and *The Wizard of Oz* and *Lawrence of Arabia* – all of which I contested (except the *Wizard of Oz*, which makes me cry every time I watch it) and then his list got silly. By the time we got to suggesting *Flubber* and *Muppet Treasure Island* and *Austin Powers' Goldmember* we were giggling a lot and I had peanut butter all down my shirt.

And then Isabel came in.

34

I'll admit I was a little tense the day Duncan arrived in Edinburgh. But then again it was our first night at the Fringe, and we'd had a four-day break from the show and travelled all the way up from London, and Patrick had had to reblock a load of scenes because the acting space was smaller, and the entrances and exits were different, and Rhia had had to drop out because her mum was ill – so there was a lot to get my head around. I needed to stay focussed. Medea is a very demanding role. So, yes, I was feeling a little stressed. But Duncan *knew* when he said he'd come, that I'd be busy with the play. It wasn't like he was expecting me to be on holiday or something. And me being pre-occupied with the play is a pretty lame excuse for what happened. I mean, aren't relationships supposed to be about supporting each other – and give and take?

To be honest, it was a little weird having Duncan there with all the NYT crowd. I suppose we'd all become quite close during the month in London – kind of like one big family. Then suddenly he was there too, and everyone was watching us. Especially Leon who, I have to say, seriously gets on my nerves.

He kept giving me these *Are-you-really-going-out-with-him?* looks as though he thought I could do a whole lot better than Duncan.

I was much more relaxed the second day, though. We went to watch a play in the afternoon and then we sat in Princes Street Gardens where all these bands were playing live. It was sunny. In between acts, Macy and Charlotte started busking, singing Avril Lavigne songs and they made one pound seventy-three in twenty minutes before a bouncer in a yellow jacket asked if they had a licence.

"Licence?" Macy said, flashing her eyelashes at him, all innocent.

"You can't busk here without a licence," the man said.

Macy pretended to be outraged. "I thought England was supposed to be a free country," she barked.

"You're not in England, lassie. You're in Scotland," the man said. "So quit your singing!" Macy took the one pound seventy-three and went and spent it on a bag of Haribo sweets that she shared out between the whole lot of us.

I was watching Duncan. He seemed happy enough, like he'd fitted in, like he was one of the gang. I was pleased he was getting on so well with everyone. And Macy – well, for some reason I'd thought they wouldn't hit it off, but they seemed to be getting on just fine. What had I been worrying about?

Duncan lined up five of those cola bottle chews along the leg of his jeans and ate them one by one.

"Duncan's in a band," I said. "Called the Posh Porpoises. They were going to play a gig at the Fringe . . ."

"You should have," said Charlotte. "It might have been your big break."

Duncan shrugged modestly.

"Do you write your own stuff?" said Leon. He said it with a *I bet you're really crap* smirk on his face which really annoyed me.

"Some of the time," Duncan said.

"They're really good," I said, staring back at Leon.

"Sing us something," said Charlotte. She handed him her guitar.

"I don't want to get moved on for not having a licence," he said, winking at me.

The guy in the yellow jacket had disappeared into the crowd. Duncan took the guitar, swallowed his last cola bottle, and started to strum.

"This is a little number . . ." he said, speaking between chords, the way Blues singers do, aping an American accent ". . . that I wrote for Isabel, here." He started to play the first few bars. "It's called *Port in the Storm* . . ."

And then he just sang it. *"You're my port in the*

storm . . ." Sitting there in the grass, completely laid back, with the guitar resting across his legs, and all of us sprawled in the sun.

When he'd finished everybody clapped and whooped and shouted "*Encore!*". He was smiling at me, that crinkly gorgeous smile. I leaned across Charlotte's guitar and kissed him.

Looking at us then you'd have thought we were a happy couple. We *were* a happy couple. I was nuts about him! So how come, only twenty-four hours later he was . . . ?

It makes me mad just thinking about it!

Can't we change the subject? Let me tell you about this medieval fort we visited today, up in the mountains? There was a siege there in 1230 and thousands of people starved to death. We sat in a café on this wiggly windy street and watched *Who Wants to be a Millionaire?* in French. How bizarre is that? And Mum bought a tablecloth. It was blue with yellow flowers . . . What? I'm boring you? Well, sorr-ee!

The day Duncan sang *Port in the Storm* was the Thursday. Saturday was our last night. I mean, the last night of the play. The last night of *Medea*. But I suppose it was *our* last night too.

Patrick had really psyched us up. There'd been a

review of our play in *The Scotsman* and the guy writing it had been really complimentary. He'd mentioned me by name: *"Isabel Bright is compelling as Medea in a performance of surprising maturity . . ."* Mum and Pete were coming up from Manchester for the final performance and Patrick said there was a theatrical agent coming to watch us. It was someone he'd invited. Someone he wanted to see our production – someone he wanted to see *me*. I was so excited! It was such an opportunity. I was about to be discovered! Okay, so it sounds silly now but what's wrong with having a dream?

After Friday night's performance I wanted to go home and sleep. We'd been out late the night before and I was shattered. Alright, so it's not my fault if I need eight hours sleep a night. Unfortunately, I'm not one of those people who can get by on a power nap and a couple of espressos. I get tetchy and weepy and stressed if I don't get enough rest. And I look all blotchy and horrid . . . Don't look at me like that! I'm not sad, I'm just sensible!

I went for a drink after the show, with all the cast and Duncan. But then I wanted to go home. Duncan said he'd come with me, but then Macy had this idea about going to a late-night comedy show. There was this stand-up gig at The Pleasance and she'd heard from someone she met at the bar that it was great. Why didn't we all go there? Even if I hadn't been tired, I probably wouldn't have fancied it that much. Macy's more into stand-up than I am. She took me to the Comedy Store in Manchester and I thought most of the acts were rubbish. And it was so smoky, it made my eyes run!

But Duncan seemed pretty keen. So they went without me. And I went home to my bed.

Are you kidding? Of course I regret it. I should have gone with them. But then, you should be able to trust people, shouldn't you?

35

MACY

In *Medea*, Jason – that's Leon, looking devastating in black leather pants – makes this speech about how marrying the daughter of the King of Corinth is an entirely reasonable thing to do. Remember, Jason's been unfaithful to Medea and he's about to get married again. (Apparently, his marriage to Medea didn't count in Corinth anyway because she wasn't a Greek! So this play is racist, too!) So he stands there and tells her that it's in everyone's best interests. Marrying the princess will enable him to raise their children (that's his and Medea's children – the ones she butchers) in the style they deserve. And, damn it, he'll be richer – so he'll be able to lavish wealth on Medea too and she can keep the house and everything! I mean, he makes it all sound so civilized. Sure, he's sleeping with someone else, but hey, he's doing it for *her* and for the good of the kids! Why does she have a problem with that? He's a good guy. He's doing the right thing by everyone.

Medea doesn't buy it of course. She calls him a filthy coward and slaps his face. Atta girl, Isabel! (You know, one night in London, she cracked him so hard that he had tears in his eyes and a woman in the audience cheered.)

It's a good try on Jason's part though, you have to admit. He's got a nerve. I could try the same approach. I could tell you that I was acting in Isabel's best interests. So here's my defence . . .

Duncan MacLeod is bad news. He's a loser – potentially anyway. He lacks drive and ambition. Isabel is the most focussed person I know. Duncan is so laid back he's practically horizontal. He'd drive her crazy in the long term. Plus he's about to go and live in Aberdeen. Aberdeen is miles away – like hundreds and hundreds of miles – and its FREEZING! Isabel hates the cold. It makes her grumpy. She'll spend all her allowance on train fares and then catch pneumonia every time she visits him. And after that? Well he's not really sure what he wants to do with his life, but maybe he'll become a writer – a poet perhaps. So he'll be penniless. And melancholy. Isabel's estranged father is a poet somewhere in France. (Not a successful one, obviously. Well, did *you* ever hear of Steve Brownlow?) And he's permanently skint and depressed. He doesn't even remember her birthdays any more! Trust me, Isabel doesn't need another failed writer in her life. So, basically, she's well out of it.

Now, all this is assuming Duncan escapes to the

mainland. The scenario could be even worse. What if he decides to stay on his island? What if he can't bear to leave Rimsay? Could you really see Isabel Bright as the wife of a fisherman? All windswept and red-faced? Covered in cow shit and smelling of lobster pots?

I tell you, I was doing her a favour!

So you think my argument doesn't stack up? You think it's bullshit! It's just as bad as the garbage Jason comes out with? You're right. So, you wouldn't believe me if I said I was acting with her best interests in mind? I bet you wouldn't. Nor should you. I'd be lying.

36

DUNCAN

If you're looking for excuses, I haven't got any.

Well, that's not strictly true. I've got a few. But they're all pretty feeble.

That I felt a little marginalised, a little peripheral, perhaps. As if I was on the fringes of Isabel's world and not really part of it. But that's just self-pity, isn't it?

That I was miffed that she went home to bed. Okay, I know. That's pathetic.

That I was horribly drunk. So that's the oldest excuse in the book, isn't it? "It wasn't me, officer. It was the alcohol! Hic!"

That it was Macy who started it . . . No, that's unfair. No smoke without fire. It takes two to tango, etc etc. I'm not going to try and get myself off the hook by blaming *her*. I'm not going to try and get myself off the hook at all, in fact.

In Shakespeare, a man whose wife has cheated on him is known as a cuckold and he has to wear horns on his head – like reindeer antlers – so everyone can ridicule him. There are all these bawdy jokes about horns – "*Are you feeling horny, my liege?*" – and it's all supposed to be so terribly funny. I don't think there's a female equivalent of a cuckold. What name do you give a woman whose partner's been unfaithful to her? Mug, perhaps? What does *she* get to wear to show everyone she's been made a fool of? Whatever it is, I don't suppose it's very funny.

I watched *Fatal Attraction* last night. Just to make myself feel better! I called in at Mr Sinclair's house on the way back from work and borrowed it from his amazing video library. I've seen it before but it was a while ago. Macy said it was one of her top ten, so I thought I'd watch it again. What? You haven't seen it? Seriously? It's a classic. That part where Glenn Close cooks Michael Douglas's kids' pet rabbit on the stove is a legendary moment in Twentieth Century cinema. It's like the shower scene in *Psycho* or Hannibal Lecter licking his lips and talking about chianti. Everyone knows about it – even if they haven't seen the film!

It was probably a bad move to watch a movie about shagging the wrong woman. Just in case you don't know the plot, I'll fill you in. Michael Douglas has a brief (very sexy) fling with Glenn Close while his wife is away for the weekend, which he then tries to write off as a bit of harmless fun. Glenn Close has other ideas and she pursues him, doing more and more desperate things until finally his nice well-adjusted wife shoots her in the bathroom (where she is lying in wait to murder him, or the wife, or both).

And there's lots of blood. But at least she doesn't butcher the kids. And there are no poisoned dresses.

I watched it at two in the morning and then fell asleep on the sofa and woke up with the dog licking my face. So now I keep expecting Macy to turn up on Rimsay and throw acid at my car. Seems unlikely, I admit. Not least, because I don't *have* a car.

Okay, so I'm joking a little. You're right – I'm being defensive. You want me to tell you how I'm *really* feeling? Well, bloody lousy actually. How did you expect me to feel? I screwed up, didn't I? I was a pathetic moron. No, worse – I was a complete bastard. Satisfied? I have this hollow sick feeling in the pit of my stomach that feels like a rat gnawing at my insides and I can't look at myself in the mirror without sneering.

So now you think I'm being melodramatic! You see, I can't win. Words are no help. They make it worse in fact. I sent Isabel some text messages right at the start – before she went to France – but she didn't reply. I don't blame her. They sounded so trivial. Now I keep trying to write her a letter – a proper letter, like the first one I sent her, after I found the bottle – but everything I say sounds crap and empty and futile. "*Sorry . . .*", "*I didn't mean to hurt you . . .*" "*It was a terrible mistake . . .*" Words are flimsy, papery things. They don't make things right again. Yesterday I wrote Isabel six letters and everyone of them ended up crumpled in the fire.

37

My big sister, Al, has gone all religious on me. Would you believe it? Alice, the most cynical person I know, has decided she believes in Jesus. She went on this thing called the Alpha Course (the one they advertise on the backs of buses with happy smiling people and a big squashy question mark) when she was at Uni and now she's started going to church. She says I should go with her to this church in Manchester that a load of students go to. Like, I don't think so, Alice! She came back from her inter-railing yesterday and she's been sending me texts. Apparently Manchester is hot, hot, hot and Alice is skint, skint, skint!

The weather has broken here. It's grey and drizzly today and there's a gale blowing off the sea. We tried playing crazy golf at a park beside the beach this morning, but the ball kept flying off-course and the palm trees were leaning over so far they looked as if they'd come crashing down on us. To be honest, I'm bored with France. I can't wait to get home. We fly back tomorrow, in the middle of the night.

Term starts next week but I'm seriously *not* looking forward to being back at school. For a start, Macy is in three out of my four subject lessons and I really can't face her. And everyone is going to be talking about it. About me. About us. Maybe I should leave. Forget the Upper Sixth. Who needs A Levels anyway? I could audition for drama school *now*. Just go for it.

Mum says theatre is too precarious. I should get a degree behind me first. Keep my options open, in case I don't make it. The agent never showed up to our last night in Edinburgh. Patrick said something had cropped up and he hadn't been able to make it. So there were no offers of movie deals. No big breaks. No instant stardom.

It all seems stupid and pointless now anyway. The future. The present. Even the past. It feels spoilt. Like everything's changed.

38

MACY

I guess if you were ranking human crimes on a scale of one to ten, murdering your children would score ten points. So would genocide and dropping the atom bomb and gassing six million Jews. But screwing someone else's boyfriend? What would that score? A two? Or a four? Or maybe even an eight? It depends on your point of view.

We wouldn't actually have gone all the way, Duncan and me. Isabel doesn't believe that. Chances are, you don't either. But, come on! We're talking snogging. Well, perhaps more than snogging. Call it petting. Heavy petting, perhaps. Making out, as we'd say in the States. But we're not talking shagging. Look, Duncan and I didn't actually DO IT! So what are you saying? That *fancying* your best friend's guy is a criminal offence? That snogging him in a reckless moment is the unforgivable sin? You've been listening too much to Isabel. She's convinced we only avoided full sex because she interrupted us. She seems to think I had it all mapped out. Like a take-over strategy.

I can't make you believe my story, but trust me, please. I didn't plan for it to happen. It was just one of those things.

And I *didn't* start it. He'll say I did. But men always say that.

39

DUNCAN

Mum phoned to tell me that Grandpa had died on the Saturday morning. The morning after the night before, if you know what I mean. My mobile woke me up. I rolled off the sofa, still in my clothes, my mouth feeling like the bottom of a parrot's cage.

"You need to come home, Duncan," my mother said. I was only half awake. My head was throbbing. In the kitchen, I was vaguely aware that Isabel and Macy were shouting at each other. I pinched the bridge of my nose to try and clear my head.

"It's Grandpa," Mum said. "He's died."

"Died?" I said, stupidly, my brain struggling to compute. "How?"

"They think he had a heart attack. I found him on the bathroom floor."

"God," I said, sinking back down onto the sofa.

After I put the phone down I just packed and left. I wasn't thinking straight. I should have explained to Isabel – about Grandpa I mean – and I should have tried to make it up with her before I went away. But she didn't exactly make it easy. The bedroom door had shut on me like the Iron Curtain coming down and when I knocked she didn't answer. I took a train to Glasgow and a bus to the airport. Mum paid for me to fly back to Rimsay. I was home by three o'clock. When I saw the stretch of sugary sand from the aeroplane window I started to cry.

How convenient? Is *that* what you think? That I used the excuse of my Grandpa's funeral to get myself out of a messy situation? That I'm playing for sympathy? Trying to divert your attention? Trying to make you feel sorry for me?

Look, aren't you getting things a little out of perspective? I know I hurt Isabel. She probably hates my guts. But she'll get over it. She'll mend.

Death is on another scale completely. It's so damn final. When someone you love goes and dies, that's it. You don't get to tell them all the things you never got round to saying. They're just gone. Finito.

There were all these birds at the funeral, flapping around our heads and shrieking as we carried his coffin to the burial ground on the headland. It was a bright sunny day. I looked up as we stood at the graveside and watched lapwings and gulls and terns whirling in the blue sky above my head. They were so free. Watching them, I realised I felt strangely free as well. The fact that Grandpa has gone and died means I can leave the island in September with a clear conscience. I won't feel bad for leaving Mum behind to look after him when I go off to university. I won't be thinking that I should have stayed to help her.

When I realised what I was thinking, I felt guilty as hell. Seems I have a lot to feel guilty about.

40

Don't tell me they wouldn't have gone all the way. I wasn't born yesterday! I know Macy Paige a lot better than you do. She was my soul mate, don't forget.

Macy pretends to be choosy and restrained, but it's all fake. Like with Phil Colvin, for example. Ages ago, back when we were doing *The Tempest*, we went to this party at Chloe Stretton's house and Macy got off with Phil Colvin. The next day she was telling me how he came on really strong to her and how she'd practically had to fight him off. Like she needed to! Phil told Jamie a completely different story. *He* said he didn't fancy Macy at all and she had thrown herself at him and was really gagging for it. He said she was a horny bitch. I hate it when guys use language like that. It's so bestial. So undignified. But that's what she is. A bitch! You see what Macy's reduced me to . . .

Whatever she says, I've got the evidence of my eyes to go on. All I know is this: I came downstairs at three fifteen a.m. to get a glass of water because my throat was dry – and Macy and Duncan were on the floor of Alice's living room together. I'll spare you the details, but let's just say Macy wasn't wearing many clothes. I rest my case.

41

How do you say you're sorry? Is it enough to say it with words or do you have to *do* something – perform some kind of atonement or make a penance? You know, do some action or series of actions that makes things better again? Something to repair the damage?

I *am* sorry about what happened. Really sorry. It was a big mistake. Isabel and me, we had a great thing going. And I blew it – just like that! I miss her a lot. She's due home from France tomorrow. I don't suppose she'll call. Maybe I should ring her. Or drop by the house?

You don't think that's a good idea? Well what would you do?

How do you mean, it depends?

What? You want to hear my version of the story? Okay, I'll tell you . . .

We were in a bar just off the Royal Mile, having a drink after the show. I met this guy who was a friend of Leon. He was over from Ireland for the Festival. He said there was this brilliant stand-up performing at a late-night gig at The Pleasance. He reckoned this guy was unmissable. His name was Ivan Hughes. He was the best thing since Eddie Izzard and everyone was talking about him. So I suggested that we check him out. Duncan was really up for it but Isabel wasn't keen. (Which was a shame. She'd have liked the gig. The guy was seriously funny, and there was a hilarious woman on after him that looked like the blonde one from *Smack the Pony*.) Isabel loved the Comedy Store in Manchester when I took her there. But anyhow she wanted to go home. She said she was really tired. So I went with Duncan. Isabel said she was fine about it. We walked her to the bus stop and Duncan kissed her and she told us to have a great time.

We were a little early, so we had a couple of beers in the courtyard out the back of The Pleasance. It was dark but there were all these strings of fairy lights and people were sitting on benches under the stars. I suppose it was quite romantic. Not that I thought that at the time. Really I didn't. Duncan was just a friend. He was my best friend's boyfriend. We were just having a laugh. It was totally innocent.

The gig was great. It was very, very funny. Duncan thought so too. I kept catching his eye. We were laughing at all the same things – which felt nice, like we were on the same wavelength. When it was over, we walked home because it was too late to catch a bus. I suppose we were a bit drunk. We were giddy and giggly. It was pretty cold. I didn't have a coat, only a top with short sleeves, so I was chilly. Duncan put his arm round me. Or did I put my arm round him? I don't remember. What? You think it makes a difference? Well anyway, it didn't mean anything. It was just a friendly way to walk on a cold night. We had a laugh about the size difference – I only came up to his belly button, he's so tall. I didn't think he fancied me at all. Why would he?

As we walked, we acted out routines from the show and we remembered the best jokes. And we talked about Isabel. Duncan said he wasn't sure what would happen when he went to Aberdeen. Aberdeen was long way from Manchester – and what about the year after, when *she* went off to uni? What would happen then? He said he hoped they'd go on seeing each other. Then he told me about this girl on Rimsay called Kate who was in his band. He said he'd had a big crush on her and they'd been seeing each other for a while when Isabel was still going out with Jamie.

"Do you still like her?" I said. We were crossing the street, passing all these tall grey houses with blacked-out windows.

"Not really," he said. "Not the way I like Isabel."

He said the way he felt about Isabel was different. Deeper.

I asked him if he loved her.

"Is it love?" I said. He was squeezing the top of

my arm, hugging me close against him as we walked along the pavement. His hand felt warm against my bare skin. He didn't answer straight away.

"Maybe," he said.

If he'd said yes, like I thought he would, it might have made a difference. It might have made me control myself more.

When we got back to the flat, Isabel was asleep. She was in Al's bed, snoring peacefully. I went up and peeped at her. Charlotte was asleep in the room next to Al's and Leon was nowhere to be seen. I remembered he'd gone off with a gang we'd met at the pub, saying he'd see us at breakfast time; so I bolted the front door.

Duncan was making toast in the kitchen. I swear that guy lives on toast! He made a slice for me too. I rummaged in the cupboard and found a jar of chocolate spread. It was real runny stuff and I had to wind the knife to stop it from dribbling off, like syrup or something. Duncan was quoting these lines from Ivan Hughes' routine – something about trombones and microwaves. I don't quite know what happened next, but somehow he made me laugh just as I was lifting the knife out of the jar, and my hand slipped, and a great big dollop of chocolate spread splattered onto my arm. On the spur of the moment Duncan leaned towards me and licked it off.

I was a little taken aback. But I have to say that it

was probably the most erotic moment of my life. The feel of his lips sent a shiver right through me and I felt all the hair stand up on the back of my neck. Before we could stop ourselves, we were kissing. Right there in the kitchen, amongst all the toast crumbs and dirty dishes.

It was a long kiss. When it finally stopped, we looked at each other – and I knew we'd crossed over into a different place and that there was no going back. Without speaking, Duncan dipped his finger in the jar of chocolate spread and wiped it across my lips. Then he kissed me again, harder and more passionately. I wish I could say I hadn't enjoyed it. And I wish I could have stopped myself. Stopped us both. My mind was racing. I tried telling myself it was just kissing. Just lips touching. It was nothing serious. It was like tasting free samples. Like trying those little morsels of food they tempt you with in the supermarket. I'd have just one more, then that would be the end. We were okay. It didn't *mean* anything. We'd kiss each other for a while and then we'd stop.

But then I was leading him into the sitting room and he was behind me, kissing the back of my neck. And we were on the sofa and he was pulling me down onto him, raking his fingers through my hair. And then we were on the floor with our arms and legs tangled deliciously and he was kicking off his shoes. And he was unbuttoning my blouse. Or was I unbuttoning it myself? Is it important? Look, it was mutual. We both wanted it.

Come on, I never meant to hurt Isabel. That sounds pretty hollow, huh?

I'm sorry. But that's not enough is it?

I need to undo what's been done. To delete it. But real life doesn't work like that. Wouldn't it be great if you could just go back and wipe over bits of your life? Rewrite them? Make them turn our differently – the way you wish they'd turned out in the cold light of day. Did you ever see that movie *Sliding Doors* where Gwyneth Paltrow's life splits in two and in one life she does one thing and in the other she does something quite different? Like she has two parallel lives. Two bites of the cherry. Two chances to get it right.

Well, in Macy Paige's parallel life – the one with the happy ending – this is what happens: Duncan and I laugh a little about the chocolate spread and I wipe it off my arm with a J-cloth and then we eat toast in the kitchen. After which I chuck a sleeping bag at Duncan and he lies chastely down on the sofa while I go to sleep in my own bed. And the next morning we're all still friends and the sun is shining.

Oh god, I wish!

42

Macy is impulsive – that's *her* problem. She'd call it spontaneous. She'd say she lives for the moment, celebrates the present. I'd say she doesn't think things through . . .

We came home from France at five o'clock yesterday morning and went to bed just as it was getting light. It was two in the afternoon when I surfaced again. Al was sitting on my bed, smiling at me stupidly and telling me she'd missed me. She had a sunburnt nose that was peeling like onion skin. I got up and had a shower and did some stretching in my room. Then I went downstairs.

In the kitchen, Alice was cooking mushroom risotto. I sat on the kitchen bench and watched her crying as she chopped onions. She started asking me about Macy. Had I sent her a postcard from France? Had I phoned her? Did I plan to phone her now I was back? Before I knew it she was giving me a lecture about "enduring friendship" and "forgiveness" and "girl power"!

"Iz!" she shrieked. "It's such a cliché that girls fall out over blokes. It's like something in one of those cheesy photostories in J17. It's like . . . God, it's like the Jerry Springer show!" She waved a kitchen knife at me. "Come on, Isabel," she said, "surely you and Macy can patch things up! She's your best mate!"

"Yeah, sure," I said. "It really *feels* like it . . ."

We ate the risotto and Alice told us stories about mad people she'd met on trains in European cities. Then we lay in the back garden on sun loungers. Alice was badgering me about going to this thing at Manchester Cathedral – some sort of "multi-sensory installation" called "Walk the Labyrinth". The word labyrinth made me think of *Lord of the Rings* and elves and trolls, and the Minotaur, and that maze at Hampton Court Palace. Somehow I couldn't quite picture this in a cathedral. But then, when was *I* last in cathedral? Maybe cathedrals had changed!

Alice said it was an "interactive prayer journey", sort of "meditating on the move". She said I'd love it. She said it was seriously mellow. That it was just what I needed to chill me out a bit – de-stress me.

"Thanks, Alice," I said, "but I don't think so."

"Honestly, Iz, you'd like it," she said.

"I'm jet-lagged," I said. "I need to unpack. Maybe another time . . ."

"Today's the last day," Al said, rolling up her top to get some sun on her tummy.

"It's now or never . . ."

Alice has this way of looking at me that I just can't resist. Well, she is my big sister after all.

So I went. To "Walk the Labyrinth." Against my better judgement. I got on a bus with Al and I went to Manchester Cathedral.

I'm not sure what I expected. I guess I'd thought it would be three-dimensional at least – you know, walls or corridors that you walked between. Caves and passageways that you could lose yourself in. It was actually just a big mat on the floor, and the mat had a pattern marked out on it with gaffer tape. It was a zig-zag pattern – all parallel lines and corners. Like those mazes you get in comics. "*Help Scooby Doo to find his way to the Scooby Snacks*" – you know the kind of thing? Dotted about on the mat were cushions and candles and weird things like a heap of stones and a tray of soil. People were walking about slowly, threading their way between the lines of tape. Or they were kneeling down or standing still. They all had Walkmans on, listening to something. Most of them looked pretty spaced out, as if they were in a trance or stoned, or zombies. Some of them had their eyes shut.

"What the hell?" I said under my breath.

"Trust me," Alice whispered. "You'll love it." I wasn't so sure.

We took off our shoes. A girl with a pierced nose and dreadlocks gave us each a Walkman and invited us to start walking. On my headset a woman with a silky voice like Mystic Meg told me to relax . . . I was going on a journey . . . I would travel to the centre of the labyrinth . . . and out again. At the centre I would meet God, my life source. Call me cynical, but I kind of doubted it.

Alice was walking in front of me, moving slowly as though she was sleepwalking. She stopped to drop a pebble into a bucket of water. I watched the ripples spread outwards. On my headset I heard some chilled-out dance music – like Moby, only not as good.

I kept walking and reached a pile of cushions beside a swing-top bin. Mystic Meg drew my attention to a pile of paper and some pens. "What hurtful things have been done or said to you?" she asked. She invited me to write or draw them on a piece of paper. No problem. I drew Macy and Duncan as stick people – like Purple Ronnie. Beside them I drew a sad face and a heart split in two. (Okay, so maybe that was milking it a bit.)

"When we forgive people, we leave these things behind," Mystic Meg purred. There it was again. The "F-word". She told me I could scrumple up the hurtful things and throw them away. I didn't need to take them with me . . . Just like that? If only life was *that* simple. Maybe Medea should have "Walked the Labyrinth"! Maybe then she wouldn't have hacked her kids to bits! She'd have just let bygones be bygones.

I did what the voice told me. I tore Macy and Duncan in half, just like the mangled heart, and I dropped them in the bin. It didn't make me feel any different.

At the centre of the Labyrinth there were more cushions and some twinkly fairy lights, like Santa's grotto. I sat down on a cushion in the lotus position and tried to feel spiritual. Alice had promised me I would feel better. That doing this would do my soul good. Mystic Meg had told me I'd meet up with God. I wasn't sure I'd know what he looked like but, hell, I was up for it . . . In the middle of the Labyrinth – the Holy Space, as they called it – the voice in my ear told me to eat bread and drink wine. There was a granary roll crumbled on a plate that looked a little stale, so I gave the bread a miss. The wine – Ribena in a big plastic tumbler – looked downright unhygienic. To the left of me, Alice was swigging away at it with a seraphic look on her face. (What *has* happened to the Alice I used to know and love? She used to be so hard to please. So streetwise. Now she keeps smiling all the time – like there's some great secret that she's just about to tell you. It's scary!)

I got up from my cushion and walked a bit further. There was a full-length mirror. *What did I see when I looked in it?* Meg asked. *Did it make me celebrate or cringe?* Well, cringe obviously. I looked sleep-starved, and my hair was all lank, and my tan was starting to fade so that I looked yellow and flaky. And my eyes looked saggy – like I'd done too much crying lately.

I hurried on to the next station and planted a sunflower seed in the tray of soil. This was supposed to make me feel connected with the cosmos – the whole circle of life thing. It didn't do much for me, I have to say. But then I always did hate biology. And soil under my fingernails? Well, that's not my idea of fun.

That just left the last station, which was a kid's sandpit. "Take off your socks and tread in the sand," said the voice on the headset. I did as I was told. The sand was cool and damp. I felt the gritty grains slip between my toes. I closed my eyes. Instantly, in my head I was on the beach on Rimsay – the one called Traigh Mhor. I was with Duncan, standing beside the pile of seaweed where he'd found my bottle. He was grinning his goofy smile at me and I was holding his hand. I was looking out to sea across the vast, smooth plane of sand that the tide had ironed flat before it slipped off down the beach. The sand looked creamy and perfect, like a golden sheet of caramel. Suddenly I started to cry . . . I thought of the beach again; only this time it was spoilt – messed up by some ugly oil spill, or churned by a million tramping feet. I thought of poisoned sea birds, of deadly toxins leaking into the sand.

Alice says spoilt things can be mended. Maybe they can. Maybe they can't.

She caught up with me, standing with my bare feet in the tray of sand, tears rolling down my face. By then I'd stopped listening to the droning voice on the Walkman and had switched it to Pause. The thoughts in my head were enough of a soundtrack for me. Al handed me a tissue from her pocket. I reckon she thought I was having a religious experience, since I was crying so much. Perhaps I was.

43

DUNCAN:

No doubt Macy told you about the chocolate spread. I don't even *like* chocolate spread that much. It was Nutella – the hazelnut stuff that tastes like the inside of those Ferrero Rocher chocolates. I don't know what possessed me to lick it off her arm! Food smearing's never really been my thing. It was the way she looked at me when she dropped the knife. If I say it was flirtatious that sounds like I'm suggesting she was asking for it, doesn't it? Which is a bit unfair. To be honest, I'm mortified when I think about what happened. I mean, bloody hell! What was I thinking of?

Don't get me wrong, Macy's a really nice girl. I mean, she's funny and I like her a lot. As a mate. But I really *don't* fancy her. Not in a "want to be in a relationship with you" sort of way. Not seriously.

I got a text from her today. When my phone bleeped I hoped it might be Isabel. Fat chance. It was Macy. The message just said: "What next?"

What next? Good question. I got my A Level results – two Bs and a C so I'm off to Aberdeen, as planned. English and Film Studies. Imagine – a degree in watching movies! Some of us have it tough!

But what next with Macy? What next with Isabel? Your guess is as good as mine. I don't reckon much on my chances.

I walked on the beach today, at low tide. There was a great expanse of fresh sand, all buttery and smooth. No marks on it. No blemishes. I thought about Isabel. (Let's be honest about this, I think about her most of the time.) I can't quite believe I messed things up so badly. When I found the bottle with the message on it, it seemed sort of magical – like a miracle. So trust Duncan MacLeod to go and foul it up! Like pissing in a rock pool! Poisoning the fish . . .

Don't you think it's interesting that Medea gets her revenge on Jason by poisoning his lover? Why didn't she poison *him*? She could have just sent *him* a poisoned cloak. Or laced his wine with something deadly, like in *Hamlet*. Maybe she thought that would be too quick. Perhaps Medea reckoned remorse was worse than bubbling to death. I wonder if Jason would have suffered more, or less, if he'd foamed and burned and melted into a toxic puddle. What d'you think? At least he'd have been dead. Which is worse – being dead or being dead guilty? What do you mean, that's a stupid question?

So, as Macy says, What next? Is Isabel going to let me stew in the juice of remorse for a while and then forgive me? Or have I blown it permanently? Has she kicked me into touch? Tell me, what should I do?

Go on texting her? Surely, she can't ignore me for ever. Or post one of my letters – even if it sounds like pants? Maybe action would be a better bet than words. Perhaps I should catch a plane and turn up on her doorstep with flowers – like Richard Gere in *Pretty Woman*. Get down on my knees and beg. Do you think she'd open the door? You think it's worth a try? When I think how I lectured her about forgiveness! "Forgiveness is as vital as air," I glibly said. What bollocks! What did *I* know about it?

I didn't tell Mum what happened in Edinburgh. I just said I'd a good time – which is undeniable, if a little misleading. If she knew I'd cheated on Isabel she'd think I was a shit. Which I am. Okay! You don't have to agree with me! I feel bad enough already . . .

Since Grandpa died, I've been being super nice to Mum. I've been hoovering and washing dishes and making a big effort not to leave wet towels on the bed. You know the stuff. The stuff mums nag you about. Mr Nice Guy. So what's going on there, then? Am I trying to make up for being a total louse in Edinburgh? Am I atoning for my sins? Or am I just making myself feel better about leaving Rimsay?

Leaving will be hard. But I'm excited. I want to tell Isabel I got the A Level results I needed. That was my first thought when I opened the envelope: *I want to tell Isabel*. Should I phone her, do you think? Will she speak to me? If I tell her, will she care?

44

MACY

If anything good came out of what happened it was Isabel's performance on the last night of *Medea*. It was a pity the agent never showed. Isabel was amazing! She was, like, SO ANGRY! Her eyes were blazing with rage and indignation. "*Passionate indignation!*" as I had to say to the other Corinthian women. Passionate indeed!

Charlotte had this line about Medea in the second scene, after her first bout of ranting about Jason. She (Charlotte) was walking amongst the audience, pointing to Medea (Isabel) – who was standing in the middle of the stage tearing Jason's clothes into long strips like bandages – and she had to say: "*Keep a safe distance. Her mood is cruel, her nature dangerous . . .*" Tell me about it! Every time I got near her on the stage she gave me these murderous looks. And later, when Jason comes to try and reason with her and she says: "*Filthy coward! This looking friends in the face after betraying them . . . it's pure shamelessness . . .*" I felt as though the words were aimed at me, not Leon.

Like you can imagine, it was an emotionally-charged performance. She didn't have to work very hard to get into character! When Isabel stood centre stage, scissors in hand, snipping a pile of letters into confetti and said: "*This blow has fallen on me . . . It has crushed my heart. Life has no pleasure left, dear friends, I want to die. Jason was my whole life . . .*" she was crying real tears. And I, standing statue-like stage right of her, was crying too. God! I wince remembering it.

When Isabel walked in on Duncan and me, at two a.m. – or whatever time it was – she didn't say a word. She didn't need to speak. The look on her face spoke volumes. It was like that moment in *Bridget Jones' Diary* when Colin Firth comes up the stairs (in slow motion) and opens the door to find Hugh Grant and his (Colin Firth's) wife naked on the bedroom floor. Except I wasn't naked. (Okay, so I wasn't fully clothed either . . .) And it wasn't in slow motion. But apart from that . . . the look of shock and disbelief and horror on Isabel's face. And the look of sheer caught-in-the-act shame on Duncan's face . . . My face? God knows what I looked like. It was only later, when I looked in the mirror, that I realised I had a smear of chocolate across my cheek. Like war paint – Mel Gibson in *Braveheart*.

Isabel stood in the doorway for a moment – her bleary-eyed sleepy look evaporating like water off hot coals. Then she turned, banged the door so hard a picture fell off the sitting room wall, and went back upstairs. Duncan ran after her. "Isabel," he shouted. "I can explain . . . it's not what you . . . God, Iz . . . I'm really sorry."

I followed after them quickly – putting my clothes back on as I went. Isabel didn't look at either of us. Didn't speak. She slammed the bedroom door (*our* bedroom door) and locked it behind her.

"Shit!" said Duncan under his breath, punching the door frame. I couldn't look him in the eye. He went back downstairs and slept on the sofa. I – since I was locked out of my bedroom – slept on the landing under a damp bath towel. I say "slept", but I don't think I actually slept at all.

It was eight-ish the next morning when Isabel came out of the room again. She stepped over me and went downstairs. I suppose she could have been excused for giving me a good kicking as she went by, or for stamping on my face or something. But that's not really Isabel's style. She bottles stuff. Very English.

I waited a few minutes and then I went downstairs too. Isabel was in the kitchen, making coffee as noisily as she possibly could. You know, kettle thumped down on the kitchen worktop, cupboard doors slammed shut, metal spoon clattering against the side of the mug, then hurled into the sink so that steel clanked against steel.

"Can we talk?" I said.

"Why?" she said, banging the coffee jar down on the shelf.

Why? Because it will make me feel better. Because I'm your friend. Because I'm really sorry. Because I hate it when you're angry with me . . . I'd rehearsed a load of reasons in my head but they all sounded limp and phoney so I said nothing.

Isabel filled the sink with hot water and started aggressively washing things and wiping down surfaces. How come anger makes people come over all tidy? My mum's like that too. When she's having a row with Dad, she scrubs things and folds things and goes all furiously house proud.

Isabel glared at me, pan scourer in hand, and said, "I trusted you! I thought you were my mate!"

"Look, Iz—" I said. She interrupted me.

"I can't believe what you did! You're such a COW!" She flung the scourer into the sink on the word "cow" and detergent foam sprayed up and stuck to the curtains.

"You fancied him all along didn't you?" Isabel said. Her voice was getting louder and louder. "All that crap about how much you liked Leon was just a smoke screen, wasn't it? It was Duncan you were after. All that, 'get him to send a photo' stuff last year – you just couldn't wait to get your claws into him, could you?"

"Look, Isabel," I said again. "It really wasn't like that—" She didn't let me finish.

"Now I know what Medea feels like!" she said, plunging a dirty pan into the water. "I know what it feels like to be BETRAYED!" She said "betrayed" in her best NYT voice – every part the tragic heroine.

That was when I made the fatal mistake. I couldn't help myself. Maybe it was the tension. I smirked. Look, I know she was pissed with me but, god, Isabel does overdo the melodrama sometimes! I'd snogged her boyfriend! Does that make me a traitor? Betrayal's a pretty strong word. Let's keep a sense of perspective here, Isabel (What? I'm sounding like Jason?).

"I'm glad you think it's funny Macy!" she said, turning her back to me.

"Look," I said defensively. "Aren't you overreacting? It wasn't what you think!"

"What do I think?" Isabel said. "That you were having sex with my boyfriend?"

"We weren't actually DOING IT!" I yelled.

"Only because I timed my entrance wrong!" she shouted.

Entrance? She really said "entrance". So even in real life she thinks she's acting in a play. This girl is losing her grip on reality. She's blurring the boundaries.

"Lighten up, Isabel!" I said. I don't know why I said that. I should have said sorry. I felt sorry. Really sorry. But I hated the way she wouldn't let me speak. And the fact that she was milking it. Being such a drama queen.

"Lighten up" is never a good thing to say to Isabel. She threw a wet sponge at me and it hit me between the eyes. Soapy water trickled down my face. I started to laugh again – at the ridiculousness of it.

"Well fuck you, Macy!" she yelled. She slammed a plate into the washing-up bowl and it cracked in two. Exit Isabel, in tears.

After that, she locked herself in the bathroom and refused to open the door. I tried pleading with her.

"Isabel, believe me . . ." I said feebly. "We weren't . . . it wasn't . . . we wouldn't have . . . Look let me in. Let me explain . . ." I seemed to have lost my ability to complete sentences. But then, what was the point of words. Whatever I said was futile. Isabel would believe what she wanted to believe. "I'm sorry," I said, finally. "I'm sorry . . . I'm sorry . . . I'm sorry!"

"Isn't it a bit late for that?" she said from the other side of the door.

Maybe she was right. But I said it again – much louder. "I'M SORRY ISABEL!"

Isabel unlocked the door. As she walked by me she said, "Talk to the hand, Macy!"

She avoided me for the rest of the day. Every time

I entered a room she exited. When I passed her on the stairs she flinched away from me, as if accidentally touching me would give her an electric shock. Like I was contagious or something. Diseased. Or poisoned.

Dunkin Donuts disappeared pretty damn quick. He just packed his stuff and got the hell out. No explanation. No apologies. No "Thank you for a nice evening!" I can't say I blame him, but it would have been nice if he'd said goodbye. Slipping away like that was pretty cowardly, in my opinion. What? You think I'm misjudging him? Well, you obviously know something I don't.

So our last day went by. Isabel was hostile. I felt like shit. Then the final performance came. And after the show we all went for a drink. Everyone was in party mood – Everyone except for me and Iz. Patrick was buying everybody drinks and telling us we were stars. You know, the usual director-speak.

Isabel wasn't drinking. She was sitting in a corner by herself, still in her Medea costume – all black chiffon and *Adams Family* eye-liner. She'd stopped ranting now. She was giving us all the silent treatment.

"Can I get you a drink?" I said. It was a long shot.

"Why?" she said, glowering at me.

"To celebrate?" I said. Yeah, like, sure Macy!

"What is there to celebrate?" she said, scowling.

"Life!" I said facetiously. "Theatre! Friendship! The end of a glorious summer!"

She didn't even answer me. She just looked at me as if I was a dog turd. Not that I blame her.

Later we went out onto the Royal Mile to watch the fireworks. They were spectacular. They crashed and screamed and splattered their colours across the sky. At one point, the whole sky was lit up with orange stars, falling in fiery fountains. I caught a glimpse of Isabel in the amber glow. She was looking at me. Staring at me with a steely glare.

45

"Does it have a happy ending?" That was what my stepdad Pete asked about *The Tempest* when we were first rehearsing it. Macy told him it was bittersweet – part happy, part sad – which is another way of saying it depends on your point of view. If you're Miranda, the ending is happy. If you're Antonio – deposed ruler of Milan - then the ending is . . . well, not so happy!

Pete had asked the same question about *Medea*. I'd been talking to him from the top deck of a bus going along Princes Street and the line was a little crackly. "Does it have a happy ending, Iz?" he'd said.

"'Fraid not," I'd said. Well I couldn't lie. It isn't a remotely happy ending. Everyone in the cast is either horribly dead or hideously humiliated. And even Medea? She might be avenged. She might have made her point. But *no way* is she a happy bunny!

"Will I need a hanky?" Pete had asked.

"A sick bag more like," I'd said, as the bus passed by Princes Street gardens.

"Shame," Pete had said. Pete likes happy endings. But then, let's face it, who doesn't?

* * *

So, my story? Does *it* have a happy ending?

Once upon a time, there were two girls who were best friends. They were inseparable – like two sides of a coin. They were a double-act. French and Saunders. Ant and Dec. Itchy and Scratchy. They were soul mates. Almost like sisters. Then one of the friends did a terrible thing. Something unforgivable. And then?

What happens next?

I'm in my bedroom. Looking at myself in the mirror. Giving myself a long hard talking to . . .

Question one: Isabel Bright, do you care enough about Duncan MacLeod to give him another chance? But hang on a minute, before I answer that there's another question: Does Duncan MacLeod actually *want* another chance? Or is he, even as we speak, happily texting Macy Paige? Inviting her to visit him in his island paradise, maybe? Writing romantic songs about her, perhaps? How will I know how he feels about me – about *her* – if I don't ask . . .

Question two (or is it three?): Isabel Bright, do you value your friendship with Macy Paige enough to put this sordid and messy incident behind you? Well, do you?

I stare at myself in the mirror, narrowing my eyes until I look mean and piggy. That one isn't straightforward either. Say for example, Macy and I kiss and make up – what about Duncan? What if Macy starts seeing him? I mean seeing him properly – becoming an item? Could I handle that? Or what if Duncan and I make up and Macy's jealous? What happens then?

Can I have *both* Macy and Duncan in my life, or do I have to choose between them? If I have to choose, do I go with girl power or true love? Which is stronger? Which matters most?

And when all is said and done, do I actually want to be friends with *either* of them?

How many questions is that? I've lost count!

But here's the clincher – the million dollar question: Does it have a happy ending?

Macy phoned me today and left a message on my voicemail. So now the ball is in my court. I either phone her or I don't. Isabel Bright – the decision is yours.

Well, go on, tell me! You've heard the story. What would *you* do?

A note from the author

When Isabel flies to the Isle of Rimsay to visit Duncan at the end of Voices their story is only just beginning. So I had to write a sequel to find out what happened next!

I was especially interested in Isabel's friendship with Macy. Just how enduring is it? How strong is the bond between two friends? And when a relationship breaks down - what then? Can it ever be mended?

Sue Mayfield is the author of Blue, Reckless and Voices.